# Sardines and Oranges

short stories from
North Africa

◆

Algeria
Egypt
Morocco
Sudan
Tunisia

Edited and
Introduced by Peter Clark

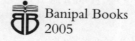

Banipal Books
2005

First published in the UK by Banipal Books, London 2005

A CIP record for this book is available in the British Library
ISBN 0-9549666-1-9

The publisher acknowledges financial assistance from the Middle East Literature Project of Westwords and the London Borough of Hammersmith & Fulham through the Strategic Initiatives funding of Arts Council England

**westwords**

Banipal Books
P O Box 22300, LONDON W13 8ZQ, UK
www.banipal.co.uk

Set in Bembo
Printed and bound in the UK by SRP Ltd, Exeter

# Sardines and Oranges

# Contents

# Introduction

## PETER CLARK

The stories in this selection are part of the modern, multi-cultural world. Pain, hardship, heartache, humour, identity, joy, loss, lack of power, and strategies for survival, are universal themes and all are represented here in tough stories that seem rooted in the authors' experiences, regardless of nationality, gender and generation.

The countries of North Africa have diverse histories but are united by a shared Arab cultural identity. Over the last century all have been subject to European occupation – Egypt and Sudan by Britain, Libya by Italy, and Algeria and Tunisia by France. Morocco was subject to both French and Spanish control. Although forty-odd years have passed since independences there is awareness of that colonial power, either as something against which to assert national identity, or as a physical refuge that can better social and economic prospects. Generally it is a collective memory, something that, in a negative way, has defined a cultural identity.

Many of the writers presented here set their stories in childhood. For some growing up was grim and short. Poverty was aggravated by patriarchal repression, whether you were a girl as in *A Red Spot* by Rabia Raihane and *Life on the Edge* by Rachida el-Charni, or a boy as in *The Tortoise* by Hassouna Mosbahi. Others look back with a gentle nostalgia, tinged with humour. Ali Mosbah recalls the myths of the rural struggle with the elements in *The Wind*. Mohammed Zefzaf in the title story, *Sardines and Oranges*, suggests that Moroccans, even as young children, were much tougher than the European colonisers and tourists.

Sometimes a distant past is seen with complex feelings through the eyes of an exile who returns, as in *The Companion* by Mohammed Dib and *Provisions of Sand* by Said al-Kafrawi. In Habib Selmi's *The Visit* the exile himself is visited by a relative from home, raising issues of memory, separation and lack of communication.

Several of the stories deal with decisive moments in people's lives at work, as they make their living. Gamal el-Ghitani in *The Crop* presents the values and traditions of rural Egypt faced with the invasion of globalisation in the form of an international hotel. Tayeb Salih lets the reader be a fly on the wall in a small and unsuccessful company, in *If She Comes*, where language, gesture and silence are observed in an office environment.

Women often have to overcome social prejudice to take menial jobs below their intellectual capacity as in Rachida el-Charni's *The Furnace*. It is not easy even to seek work as in *Bad Soup!* by Latifa Baqa. The socially marginal – servants, prostitutes, flower sellers – struggle to maintain dignity and a quality of life against all odds, even putting their lives at risk. This is a world that Mohamed Choukri has excelled in writing about: his story *Men have all the Luck* is raw and powerful, with no happy ending. These themes of archaic, unjust and brutal social relations, are explored, too, by Sabri Moussa in *Sa'diya Fell from the Balcony*. Being too much out of step with the authorities can also lead to meaningless imprisonment as in *The Sweetest tea with the Most Beautiful Woman* by Tarek Eltayeb.

Only one of the stories in this collection, by the late Mohammed Dib, is translated from French. Writers under foreign occupation used to face both cultural and linguistic challenges. Many from countries that had been under French control had no choice but to write in French and have contributed to the literature and culture of mainland France. But since independence all countries have expanded education and today literacy among the younger generation is nearly universal. Writers have responded to this and write for a new Arab readership. Shared experiences are articulated.

But contemporary Arab literature still operates within glass barriers. A converging pan-Arab culture is developing in Europe, away from local patrons and censors, but still Arab writers tend to be read in the main only by Arab readers or, in translation, by their sympathisers. Very few Arab writers have been able to achieve the world recognition of, for example, South American writers. This is unfortunate for, as the stories in this collection reveal, all have resonance far beyond the confines of the Arab world.

But changes are afoot. Writers from all over the Arab world come and go, and some settle in Europe. Iraqis, Tunisians and Moroccans, for example, get to know each other's work in Paris and London in a way that did not happen twenty-five years ago. Now knowledge of the contemporary Arab world is extending to the rest of the world. Mainstream publishers are still wary of publishing translations of contemporary Arab literature, but this should not allow us to disregard the great progress that has been made.

Since it started in 1998, *Banipal* magazine has become a major medium of access to contemporary Arabic literature. It has maintained both quality and independence. It has brought to the attention of the interested Anglophone reader works of both established authors and the major writers of tomorrow.

*Banipal* is now publishing in book form selections of translated work that first appeared in the magazine. This collection is the first in the series, and celebrates the short story of North Africa. As in the magazine, this selection contains work by both established and emerging authors. As in the magazine, the criterion is significance and quality.

*Banipal*'s international range is illustrated by the backgrounds of the translators of this collection. Only four of the thirteen originate from the United Kingdom. Others are based in Canada, Jordan, Morocco and the United States. The translators are from Arab, British and East Asian backgrounds. Translation knows no frontiers and has become an aspect of a global culture.

Whatever the approach of the author – through autobiographical sketch, philosophical reflection, nostalgia or grim realism – this selection shows that contemporary writing from North Africa possesses a vitality we need more of. Like the iceberg, what we see is only a fraction of what could be translated. The work of *Banipal* has only just started.

*January 2005*

# A red spot

## R A B I A   R A I H A N E

To join the girls in their afternoon play means for me to change into a free bird, whose insides are bristling with a strong desire to fly here and there, or to hide just like a wild rabbit or a restless gazelle that knows how to enjoy being free in a wide open space.

While I was still a young girl of fourteen – an age at which I was supposed to show obedience to my parents as well as timidity – my mother decided she was going to marry me off. It happened because one of our distant relatives, who had visited us unexpectedly, could not lift her eyes off me when she saw me, head bowed and looking at my feet, carrying out to the letter my mother's commands and explicit instructions. Prompted by her intuition, which was never wrong, she told my mother that I'd make a good wife for her son.

Confused, I felt as though I had grown up fast into a full woman when my sister broke the news to me. My mother's face beamed with joy: I would have a husband, unlike my aunt's daughters. But when the subject was mentioned in the presence of my father I became very shy and embarrassed.

However, by sunset, I had already completely forgotten about the matter. Halima had peeped round the door – our door which is never shut. "Come and play!" she said. So I joined her, but after hopping for two squares, I stopped playing and withdrew to a corner. She called my name out several times, and when I did not respond, she walked away:

"May God strike you down, you rotten thing!"

What's happening to me? I remembered the policeman's daughter and her domineering mother. I also recalled the frightened women, some of whom had become spiteful and begun to rejoice at other people's misfortunes. A terrible thing had happened in the policeman's household: his beautiful daughter's handsome bridegroom left her. He just opened the window, in the dark, and jumped out. That gave our mothers a good excuse to call us all in and to reprimand us – from the youngest girl to the oldest one amongst us.

"You girls bring shame and disgrace upon us!" they said.

The policeman's daughter was not a virgin. Shocked senseless when he found out, the bridegroom, feeling betrayed, left her. Her mother retreated into a corner and began slapping her cheeks. Her father got on his motorbike and drove off. No amount of consolation was any help. As for the bride, she just sat there, helpless and vulnerable. Wicked tongues said it was a logical consequence of all the wrongs her parents had done other people: her father, the policeman, was rude and cruel and had a heart of stone, sparing no one with his belt or stick; her mother, emboldened by her husband, bubbled with evil and wickedness.

The women made fun of the policeman: "He was too busy watching others," they said, "he should have been watching over his daughter's virginity!"

We girls grew even more anxious and worried. We'd meet and talk. We were wondering where all that astuteness had come from, all that wisdom which we discovered was our shield against losing our virginity: avoiding jumping too high, sitting on anything that had a sharp edge, and peeing where boys urinated.

My heart pounded from fear whenever older girls asked us younger ones to stick out our tongues – that was their way of taking revenge upon us: "You're a virgin." "And so are you!" "You're a virgin, too!" "No, you're not!" they would tell each one of us as they "examined" our tongues. Imagine the distress we had to endure from that disgusting way of telling who was a virgin from who was not, even if it was just a crazy game.

We had never experienced sex but we had thought about it a great deal. Our mothers' warnings against having sex, and their admonishments, were like the tolling of bells they rang without cease, which dampened our desire for it altogether.

Mariam lost her virginity behind an unfinished building.

I was not her friend. She was a little older than me, and she was too busy looking after herself and her siblings; maybe because she was the oldest, her mother shifted the burden of looking after them from her shoulder to her daughter's.

Mariam's brothers were keepng a low profile; they could no longer draw self-assurance from their father, the policeman, or from their own physical strength. They knew that they were the talk of the town, reviled and condemned – the kind of response one attracts from people when one commits a sin.

The idea that Mariam's family would not let this humiliation go unpunished was in the air; the women even brought to mind the father's pistol and the brothers' big knife. But due to a certain divine wisdom, the father and the brothers heeded the old women's talk and their good offices, and abided by the saying *"Fate and the Divine Decree* – you want this, and I want that, but God does what He wills."

The town revelled in the gossip about the policeman's daughter until people eventually lost interest in her story. Mariam kept herself out of sight, becoming meek and totally submissive. She was the household's very obedient slave.

When my mother broached the subject of my marriage to my cousin with me, her face radiant with joy, I stammered and burst into tears. Mariam's beautiful face loomed in my mind. I imagined her alone, kneeling, cleaning and scrubbing, being violently abused by everybody, and accepting it all.

I implored my mother: "I don't want to get married. I really don't."

"But I want," she said.

"Then you marry him!" I retorted, feeling rather disconcerted. I held my head bowed for some time, and when I raised it to look at her, I saw her face had turned ashen at my response, but she soon regained her calm, saying: "He's nice and rich."

My face contorted with pain as I said, threatening: "If you force me to marry, I'll run away."

My answer seemed to stun her and she sat there brooding. Then I heard her say in an aggrieved voice: "Why would you do that?"

"Because I don't want to be anybody's slave!" I said, full of anguish and staring hard at a red spot on the tiled floor.

*Translated by Ali Azeriah*

# Life on the Edge

## RACHIDA EL-CHARNI

After we had let the sheep out of the barn and taken them to the pasture next to our fields, we heard the voice of our mother warning us:"Don't go too far, it's going to rain soon."

Invigorated by the return of the warm sun after a few grey days, the sheep moved quickly, pushing each other gently forward. As they grazed they spread out through the pasture, watched by our vicious dogs. My two brothers, Ammar and al-Amin, played with a ball made of old socks while I lay on the tender grass smelling the scent of spring and basking in its splendour.

The hills that surrounded us were bordered by high mountains, which we considered to be the end of the world. We believed that the hereafter, the world where hell and heaven existed and where God judged the dead surrounded by His Angels, lay behind them. Our parents' warnings to us to stay close confirmed our suspicions. As I gazed at the mountains, examining their height, I wondered to myself why I should not go to the end of the world and eavesdrop on the inhabitants of the hereafter? I felt that at the age of ten I should be able to conquer my childhood fears more than at any other time. I called my brothers and discussed the idea with them. At first a deep sense of fear ran through their every pore, then al-Amin, the elder of the two, agreed to join me in my adventure. We left Ammar to guard the sheep and walked toward the nearest point that would lead us up the mountains.

We walked for a long time but the mountains seemed even higher, which made us feel that the hereafter was quite far. Dark clouds began to gather behind the mountain peaks, filling me with fear as they formed shapes of strange creatures, menacing us with cruelty and anger. I thought of this as a warning message from the inhabitants of the hereafter and my heart was thumping with terror. When I suggested to my brother that we go back he agreed immediately. His lack of enthusiasm, which he tried to hide, comforted me. There was a sudden and very heavy downpour, and soon everywhere was deluged with rain. We ran with all our might as we were concerned about the sheep. When we reached Ammar we found him trying to round up the flock with a small stick.

We herded the sheep together, making them move as fast as possible to avoid being caught in floods from the nearby valley of Majrada. The muddy ground through which we were all stumbling hampered the movements of the ewes and the lambs. As we approached the house we could see my mother's anxious face. She wore boots and had covered her head with a woollen shawl, and was trying to hide her advanced stage of pregnancy. She was so worried about us that she was really very angry. Her reaction to what we had done was motivated by her fear of my father's harshness in all matters concerning his sheep. He was very attached to them and was more saddened by any illness among them than by the death of a relative.

As we herded the sheep into the barn my father arrived back from the village. He started hurling insults at us when he discovered they were wet. I do not know how, but he also quickly discovered that some were missing. We glanced at his angry face and trembled with fear as he counted his sheep. His voice thundered: "You devils, I will kill all of you tonight. Two ewes and three other sheep are missing. Where are they? Where did you lose them? How could you fail to guard them? Oh, my ruin! Oh, my shame! Go and look for them – and do not come back until you find them."

Fear pinned us to the ground and we could neither talk nor even raise our eyes to look at him. When he realized that we were paralysed with fear he grabbed a stick and came towards us, threatening to kill us all. We ran from him, leaving our mother to plead with him in a trembling voice: "It's getting dark and it's raining, they can search for them in the morning." To which our father replied: "Stop, or I will send you out with them. You let them go out. You're responsible for what happened. You are bad luck!"

We left the house and walked towards the pastures where the sheep had grazed earlier. We took small and careful steps, stumbling as we felt our way over ground that was saturated with water and where large pools had formed. We searched for the lost sheep in the hills and among the trees, but to no avail. By nightfall we were weighed down by fatigue, and our fear and confusion increased as it became difficult for us to see through the heavy, incessant rain. It seemed the rain was going to flood the whole world.

We walked back home, preparing ourselves for the dreaded confrontation with our father. We were scared to death as we walked slowly towards the house. We soon saw our mother holding a storm lamp and calling on us to come inside. We were dripping wet and shivering from fear and cold as we entered the house with our heads bowed.

When my father saw us returning without the sheep he came towards us full of anger. He unbuckled his leather belt to give us a thrashing. We tried to escape his grip but he came after us and beat us; even my pregnant mother, who was trying her best to protect us, was not spared. That night we fell asleep to the sound of our sobbing and my mother's crying.

❧

I do not know how much time elapsed before I woke to the frightening wailing of my mother's cries which soon turned to exhausted moans. Worried, I asked her: "Mother! What's wrong?"

"I think I'm about to give birth, but don't worry, my daughter, I'll wait until the morning."

I could not get back to sleep with the anxiety taking hold of me as I listened to my mother's moans that occasionally erupted into loud screams. Eventually she told me to find my father and ask him to fetch the midwife or call her parents.

My father was in the habit of retiring to the barn whenever he was angry. He would abandon us for days, sleeping near his animals that he liked and considered more faithful and dearer to him than his family and friends. I felt my way to where he was sleeping and touched his feet, saying: "Father, wake up! Mother is in pain, I think she's about to deliver."

He replied with total indifference: "She couldn't have picked a better night than this one to give birth?"

"Please, Father," I begged. "Go to her parents and tell them about her condition."

"I will not go out now, it's still raining. Let her wait till morning."

I returned to my mother, where I found Ammar and al-Amin awake and staring at her in bewilderment. As I repeated to my mother what my father had said, I felt embarrassed by his attitude. She controlled her pain and turned to the handloom, holding it firmly to help avoid raising her voice, which would have scared us.

I continued to watch the expression on her tired face. As her screaming spells filled my ears, I realized that she would certainly give birth before morning. I went back to my father, begging him to go and see her, but he refused adamantly, saying: "That is women! Spoilt!"

"Please, Father," I insisted. "She's in real danger and might die."

His reply was worthy of an enemy as he said: "Let her die, her life is cheaper than the sheep she's made me lose."

His vindictiveness shocked me. I left disappointed, and wondered whether this was truly my father and how I could have been born to a man who had no conscience. In my

18

mind I could find no excuse for his conduct. I decided that from then on I did not need him. I did not need such a heartless father. His wrath and anger had swept away all feelings I held for him and destroyed them with this final blow, plunging me into a profound state of sadness. Drying my eyes, I felt ashamed to be his daughter.

I met al-Amin near the door on his way to try and convince Father to help Mother. I told him that it was useless, but he insisted on talking to him. He soon returned defeated, took his coat and announced in his nervous, childish way, his decision to go to his grandfather's house. In her weak voice, my mother tried to stop him but he insisted on going and ran out of the house feeling his way in the dark and the rain.

My mother's cries resonated in the stillness of the night, filling me with anxiety. Her pale face scared me. I was confused; I did not know what to do to help her. I searched my mind trying to recall matters related to life and birth, but I could only remember the hot water that the midwife took to my mother's room when she gave birth to Ammar. I put water on to boil and no sooner had I done it that I heard her weak, plaintive voice calling me: "Bring the scissors and disinfect them with alcohol."

I did what she asked, wrapped the scissors in a clean towel and placed them near her. I also told her that I had boiled some water.

I watched her suffer with the anxiety of the helpless. She walked back and forth in the room and later lay down. I helped her cover herself. She then raised her arms, held the posts of the bed behind her head, and opened her legs. She asked me to press hard on specific parts of her stomach and guided my little hands to where they were needed. I felt a movement inside her, making me wonder how much she was suffering. Her beautiful face had turned blue like the sky on a dark night as she tried to suppress her cries and to breathe deeply in order to push the child out into the world. Finally, in the midst of her pain she asked me to get the hot water quickly, and prepare the baby's clothes.

As I was bringing the water I heard angelic cries. I rushed back with the water and when I entered the room I was surprised to see the baby near my mother. She had been able to cut and tie the umbilical cord. She had placed him under the covers to provide him with her blessed motherly warmth.

*Translated by Aida A Bamia*

# The Tortoise

## HASSOUNA MOSBAHI

That was my first adventure. Before that adventure and afterwards, until I was a fourteen-year-old adolescent, they used
to beat me with a nail-studded stick that sometimes drew
blood. There was another stick, more slender, cut from olive
or oleander. It twisted like a leather belt and marked my back
and thighs with red or violet weals. With each stroke it hissed
with pleasure or revenge – "Ayyah". When I look back today
I wonder how I managed to survive.

They used to beat me all the time. At funerals and on feast
days. When it was cold, and during the afternoon siesta. Only
when they were tired or bored did they give up. There I
would be, mouth agape, bloody, unable to shout or cry
because of the acute pain. Everyone took part – Father,
Mother, my sister Bayyah, uncles, aunts. Even distant relations used to have a go. They said they had to make me worthy of the family name and fit to be my grandfather's grandson. He had been a noble knight, well regarded by plain and
mountain, a man to whom the tribes of west and east bowed
in reverence.

When the blows were raining down on me I secretly
appealed to him. Perhaps he would deliver me from this awful
pain. In writhing agony I imagined him arriving suddenly on
horseback, brandishing a sword in their faces, shouting:
"Leave the boy alone, you swine!"

They would turn tail, crushed. I would then stand at his

side, triumphantly watching their retreat.

But he remained silent, like the distant mountains that surrounded our village. The earth remained the earth and the sky
the sky, the same as ever. With the passing of time and the
increase of pain I grew to hate him as I hated them. Indeed
more than once I felt he was behind them, blessing their
deeds and spurring them on in their abuse of me. When I
passed the cemetery I decided to go and piss on his grave. As
I did just that my whole body burnt and my head boiled like
a cauldron. It was as if the soil was grumbling and the heavens were mumbling in fury, like some wild beast touched by
evil. I then ran off, trailing clouds of rust-coloured dust.
Thenceforth he occupied an obscure place in my heart and I
grew to fear him as one fears ghosts or the worthy saints of
God.

They all beat me. Father did it almost every morning.
Sometimes he would bind my arms and legs and throw me
into the barn all day or all night without food or drink. Or
when I was some distance from him he would throw his stick
at me as if I was some frisky or obstinate beast of burden. He
would constantly say I was worthless or was the son of a dog,
and his moustache would quiver like a thorn bush. I sometimes thought as I wandered among the olive fields in the
autumn that I was perhaps not his son. Had I been found in
some ditch or by the roadside? I had in mind a story told by
al-Khatimi, Mother's brother. The central character was a
child, abandoned by his mother near some village, who then
fled to the mountains and lived a tough life, full of hardship
and tears.

When I thought of that legend my sense of individuality
grew. The world extended before me, dry and sad, filling my
mind with fantasies and whisperings. I would sit under an
olive tree, my head leaning against the trunk. I would sob and
sob, no longer able to see what was in front of me.

Mother used to beat me before I went to bed and at meal-
times. Sometimes she would chase me, stick in hand, through

olive fields, valleys and on the plain surrounding our village. When she got tired she would throw herself on the ground, sweating, with dry lips and shouting to anybody around: "Grab him, the son of a dog. He's brought distress to his parents."

And Bayyah was my sister. She and I slept in the same bunk. I would go with her to the spring, to the olive fields, to the harvest. We gathered straw for the pack animals together. She showed me no pity and used to devise ways of beating me more than the others. Once she put my head between her thighs and smacked my bum until it felt as if it was on fire. And once she pummelled me like a lump of dough. She then sat on top of me and pushed down and down until the whole of my body was one big scarlet bruise. She used to pinch my ears so I had a fever at night. When she pinched my cheeks it was like a scorpion's sting in the heat of August. I hated her most when she tried to be like Mother, even more so when she stiffened and pursed her lips and stuck her nose in the air like some stern old lady. If only she were smaller than me, I would have exacted my revenge and thrown her onto the fire. I thought of killing her when she was sleeping in the bunk one hot afternoon, the flies buzzing around her, drawn by the smell of milk coming from her mouth. But some movement outside made me change my mind, I went off in anger to the olive fields.

On one occasion I did feel affection for her. She sang me a song she had memorised after some outsiders came to the village, erected some red flags and told us, "Rejoice. We are now independent." They all stood in a row and sang the song, with fists raised high. They then set off for the west, still singing, and stamping the ground in their black shoes, disappearing into the woods, their voices apparently suspended in space.

Bayyah used to sing this song as she followed the cow to pasture on spring mornings, full of light and sweet smells. All day she would sing, "Protectors, protectors, the glory of our age". And she would stamp the ground with her bare feet. Sometimes I would see her wander far away. She would blush and stare at the scrubland in the west. On that day I felt affection towards her and would like to have kissed her and hugged her. I wanted her to call me, put me on her lap and promise never to hit me again. But that evening as we came near our house she threw herself on me suddenly, and seized me by the neck as you seize a chicken when you are about to kill it. She then squeezed my neck so tightly that my tongue fell out as far as it could go and I felt as if my eyes were popping out. Mother then savagely called out: "Go on, hit the dog until he gets things right."

Today when I call on her, she shows me the latest carpet she has woven. Her seven children crowd round me and she tells them: "Look, this is your uncle. I've told you all about him. Look at him and be like him."

She then turns to me and says: "If I thought you'd turn out like this I wouldn't have hit you so much."

I looked back and she was almost in tears.

"Forgive me, brother," she said. "I did love you, but I wanted you to be a man, a lord of men, as you've now become."

I stayed a day or two and then moved on. She stood still in her faded red dress, bidding farewell, her eyes full of tears of anguish.

They all beat me. None of them showed me the slightest compassion, or gave me a kind word, even accidentally. They took pleasure in abusing me and abasing me, as if I were the cause of their hunger and thirst, the drought and their oppression, of the diseases of the olive trees and the beasts, the death of the wild figs before they had matured, and the other calamities that afflicted them over the years. All, that is except my aunt Fatima, who showed kindness and decency. She had a tattoo on her forehead and would kiss me when we met in the dry river bed, in the olive fields or at the spring.

When I went to call on her she would give me some sweets and some Turkish delight and lots of other things. She would put my head on her knee and trace her fingers in my hair, looking for lice. When she found one she would kill it glee-fully. She cursed Mother for her treatment of me, and Father for thinking only of his beasts and his animals. I hugged her and wanted to stay with her for ever. I once went to see her. She was grinding corn. She sat me beside her and sang to me:

> *Oh, my gazelle, I have brought you up.*
> *How beautiful you are with your jet-black eyes.*
> *This alone shows God's power*
> *And has led me to you.*

I felt that I was that black-eyed gazelle, wandering at liber-ty, browsing in valley and plain, without restraint and allow-ing nobody to come near. She would then sing other songs that transported me to distant lands, and filled my heart with loneliness and sadness. I would imagine I was a blade of grass in a raging storm. I then came to myself. Aunt Fatima was there, sobbing. I too was in tears, my head on her knee. When I went home that evening I felt that I and my aunt were outsiders in that cruel village.

Nowadays when I call on her I find her in a corner, shrunk and sightless. I approach her in silence. She feels me and smells me, and then repeats my name and throws herself at me, weeping and saying: "Where are you, my fair gazelle? I have been told that you have crossed the seas and have gone to Frankish lands. What are you doing there? I always knew you were a bright lad. You do not forget us, my boy, you are a piece of my own flesh and blood."

That was my first adventure! Before that adventure and afterwards, until I was fourteen they would beat me and call me foul bastard, ass, Ibrahim's donkey – this Ibrahim was a neighbour who had a wretched obstinate donkey with a back that bled all the time. They called me mule's hoof, bitch's whelp, dung beetle and . . . many other things I have now forgotten. They would fall like stones on my mind, scald my body like knives and fill my soul with pitch. Sometimes I would take Mother's small round mirror and hide in the barn for an hour or so, gazing at the reflection of my face, with all these epithets mingling in my mind so it all became an ugly obscure mass. I then wept bitter tears, wishing I might never leave the barn.

Once I saw my face in a muddy pool and almost cried out in fright. It was broad and dry like barren land or like the stones of cruel mountains. There were lines of snot and tears and furrows of pain and confusion. And one afternoon when I stretched out under an olive tree I saw Ibrahim's donkey surrendering itself as usual to the heat and flies. I went to look at it sympathetically and then I found myself – I don't know how – at its side, talking caressingly to it. But it paid no attention to me and stayed still, gloomy-eyed, loath to contemplate its own ugliness or the ugliness of the world around.

They used to beat me and say: "May God gouge your eyes out. May He make your children childless. May He slam every door in your face and blacken your reputation and scatter every path you take with thorns. May you die in some remote mountain pass."

When they got tired of this or ran out of other misfortunes to wish for me, they would raise their hands and call on the Prophets and God's worthy saints to answer their prayers. There would be no rhyme or reason for these curses. They would say: "Why are you quiet all the time? Don't you have a tongue?"

When I spoke they would say: "Why does your tongue go round and round like a fan?"

When I was up early,

"Why are you first up like a cock?"

And if I stayed up late with them,

"Do you want to learn bad habits, you bastard?"

If I smiled, "Why do you laugh all the time as if we had no

clothes on?"

And when I frowned, "Why are you always glum and gloomy? Do you want to court misfortune for us?"

And so it went on. That is how things were with me. One morning I was recalling those days in the English Gardens in Munich. I began to laugh aloud and stamp my feet. Two old ladies were sunbathing in the warm April sunshine. A girl walked by exercising her dog. She was like a tailor's model in a shop window. Then there was a punk who was like an old hoopoe bird, laughing and spitting all the time. I laughed even more, and people scattered in alarm. The punk sat there some distance away and stretched out his legs like a dog at ease, breathlessly waiting for things to happen.

That was my first adventure.

Before then I used to wander in the fields and woods. I could capture jerboas in their lairs and surprise rabbits as they slept with open eyes and trap birds in their nests. I would spend ages doing these things. I would listen to noises, know when the olives turned black, when the almonds had bloomed, when the wheat yellowed with the ears nodding, when the wild figs ripened and turned red. I got depressed by the distant mountains that towered over our village in all directions, preventing me from seeing what was beyond. When people travelled east or west or north or south my heart went with them. When people talked about strange worlds filled with light and sound, with sweets and cakes I felt restrained and yearned to fly beyond the mountains. I memorised the names of the cities and villages they talked about. I repeated them to myself, intoxicated and breathless. I cursed those mountains. They were alongside the people who beat me and humiliated me all the time.

From the beginning I seemed strange and odd to my family. I hated watering the fields, getting hay for the donkeys or Indian figs for the camels. Whenever I did these chores I always feared the stick and the abuse. When I undertook any of these tasks I would make some mistake so they would think

I was just daft, some dumb clown unfit neither for the world nor for religion, that I was some misfortune from which they suffered.

My happiest time was when I was stretched out beneath the olive tree gazing at the beauty of the heavens. Or when I disappeared into the barn, taking some charcoal to draw on huge copper pots shapes and lines like those I had seen on the writing-boards of the boys as they returned from the house of the schoolmaster.

At home they used to say that my uncle Mohammed had studied at the Zaituna Mosque in Tunis. They held him in awe and often sought his advice in matters of God and of man. He would walk with them, tall and broad, his tummy stuck forward and his fez tilted back and a cigarette always between his lips. But Father also said crossly that uncle Mohammed had all but impoverished the family and broken it up. They had sold six cows so he could become a respectable man of letters, bringing honour to the family. But he failed in his studies because of some snub-nosed woman from a western tribe whom he fell for. For her sake he came back to the village with huge trunks full of books and papers. I would look at these trunks, trembling with a desire to know what they contained.

One day, thanks to the carelessness of the snub-nosed wife, I opened one of them and took out the first book I touched. I hid it under my djellaba and went off behind the cow. Father shouted at me, telling me to make sure the cow did not trample the crops. But as soon as I could I stretched out on my tummy under the warm spring sun. With shaking hands I opened the book and gazed with wonder at its lines and images. I soon forgot the world and what was in it. My mind wandered among lands that were violet and sky-blue, or the colour of red anemones. I was oblivious of everything until I felt a stick on my body and heard Father shouting and swearing at me. But for an elder of the village passing by he would have killed me that day. That night before I went to sleep he said to me: "Listen, my boy, do you want to ruin the family like your uncle Mohammed did? If I come across you again with those books and papers in your hand I will roast you alive."

But I soon forgot his threats and went back to gazing at those trunks, my eyes glistening with desire, eager to know their contents.

One day I was looking after the cow as usual, and some lads came along carrying their writing-boards. I looked after them as they squawked like happy chicks and then I found myself – I don't know how – following them. Suddenly I noticed a cousin, slightly older than me. He shouted at me like one of the grown-ups: "Go back to your cow, boy!"

When he went on threatening me, I picked up a stone. "Listen to me," I shouted. "Leave me alone or I'll smash your head in."

Perhaps he thought I was serious, for he then ignored me. I went with them all to the schoolmaster's house, entered and squatted down like the rest of them. Soon their heads rocked to and fro and they mouthed those wonderful words. Then Father came in like a raging bull, with his stick, crazy and menacing. He said nothing to the schoolmaster, totally ignoring him.

"Here, you dog," he shouted.

My cousin stood up, finding the chance of exacting revenge on an enemy, and pointed at me.

"There he is, uncle, in the corner," he said. "I told him to go back but he threatened me with a big stick."

I recoiled with terror and looked appealingly to the schoolmaster. My lips trembled and I was on the verge of tears. I saw a glint of sympathy in the schoolmaster's eyes, like a bird in the distance. Before Father could reach me the schoolmaster seized his hand and led him gently to the door.

"Shame on you, Ibn Ali. Are you forbidding your son from learning the word of God?"

"The boy will bring you pain and distress," Father shouted.

29

"He has no idea what is behind him or what is in front of him. He's a disaster I've had to suffer from."

The schoolmaster put his hand on my shoulder.

"Leave him in my care," he replied. "Who knows? He may surprise us all."

For the first time I saw Father crushed. The stick was lowered. His eyes wandered awhile and he left, head somewhat bowed.

A few months later my cousin was having trouble reading one of the suras of the Qur'an. The schoolmaster's stick hovered over his head. My cousin froze like a mouse surprised by a cat, his lips quivering in search of the forgotten verse. When I felt he was lost I repeated the verse. I blushed in spite of a sense of elation I felt for the first time in my life. The other boys turned in my direction like calves that had been brought their feed. The schoolmaster lowered his stick and looked at me. There was astonishment in his features.

"Go on," he said.

And I went on, rocking forward and back. I continued and did not stop until I had finished the sura. He asked me to recite another sura. I did so without concern or hesitation. When I finished he gave praise to God and dismissed the other pupils. He took me by the hand and we walked in silence to our house. As we approached I could see Father stitching his smock, his stick at his side and a pot of tea before him. When he saw us he shouted: "Now you know the son of a dog. I told you he was useless, fit only for a beating, didn't I?"

I tried to hide and clung to the schoolmaster's cloak. I waited for Father to jump up with his stick. But he remained engrossed in his stitching, muttering something I could not make out. We stood in front of him.

"Did I not tell you that your son would surprise us?" the instructor said proudly.

Father stopped stitching, looked up but said nothing.

"Listen, Ibn Ali," the instructor continued. "For twenty

years I have been teaching the Qur'an around the place, but never have I come across a pupil like your son. Just imagine, he has learnt every sura just by listening."

He then repeated Surat al-Waqi'a to him. To prove his words he asked me to repeat it. I sat down, did so, and we wandered from sura to sura, my face pink, my head rocking.

But this incident changed nothing. They went on beating and abusing me until I was fourteen years old.

That was my first adventure.

That incident took place in the autumn when the village enjoyed itself. There was a togetherness among the people, who had happy, laughing, radiant faces. The rains at the end of August had banished that ugly barrenness that followed the harvest. Wild figs covered the ground with their lovely russet coat. Every night the plains and the hills echoed to the rhythm of drum and pipe, the chanting of women, the songs of the men and the firing of guns. At sunset the alleys were full of the bustle of excited young people as they went from wedding to wedding, looking for eyes that would burn their hearts in daytime.

One autumn day I was lying beneath the olive tree, dreaming as usual and contemplating the beauty of the world. Suddenly Ugly Salih was standing before me and asking me what I was doing.

The grown-ups were always telling us not to pass by blood or ashes without saying, "In the name of God". We were to shun the valley, fire, camels and not go near Ugly Salih. He was evil, disobedient, filthy and had a huge mouth.

I sat up ready to defend myself or to flee. I don't know why they called him "Ugly". Mother used to say that his family ate grass and wild figs, and that his father lost everything through gambling and quarrelling, and that his mother was a prostitute. Amazing stories were told about him. They said they found him once in the village of Makthar, and once in the village of Hajib al-'Ayun. Once he boarded a bus and went to Kairouan. I also heard them say he had stolen a chicken from el-Askari and a turkey from el-Muldi, and that he had split open el-Gharbi's head with a stone. All this went through my mind while his lips shook continuously. But not a sound did he utter.

Again he surprised me.

"Listen," he said. "Do you want to come with me to al-'Ala? It's market day tomorrow. If you like we can go at dawn and get back in the afternoon. Nobody will take any notice of us."

He described the market, and the donkeys, the sellers of hides and eggs, the vegetables, the crowded buses. "You're on your way to cities far away where you have cars — red, green and yellow, making a noise like women celebrating. We can eat honey-cakes and buy sweets and that white bread our families sometimes get."

He went on talking and talking. My mouth opened wide with amazement until a fly found its way in and I was throwing up for an hour, feeling that my whole stomach was turning into one great black fly that carried the filth of the world.

Ugly Salih remained at my side, whispering. He seemed to be kind and good. He then took me again by surprise.

"Let's go and find a tortoise," he said.

"A tortoise?"

"Yes, a tortoise. They fetch a high price at the market, you know."

He put his hand into one of his huge pockets and brought out a handful of change.

"I've still got this left from the money I got from selling a tortoise last Thursday at al-'Ala."

I was dazzled and imagined that for the price of a tortoise I could buy the whole world. I saw myself coming home from al-'Ala with white clothes and black shoes like those men who came to the village and unfurled flags and then set off west, singing that beautiful anthem. The bad stories I'd heard about Ugly Salih vanished from my mind and I followed him without hesitation.

We wandered through valleys and scrubland. We climbed up and down, and went so far that we could see nothing of the village. We looked down on other villages that seemed sad and empty. I was afraid and wanted to go back. He reassured me, his eyes fixed firmly on the ground. We went so far that my legs ached and my throat was dry. The sun was sinking rapidly towards the western mountains, and twilight was cloaking the lower plain and the deeper valleys. Suddenly from behind a cypress tree his voice came to me: "I've found them. I've found them."

I hurried up to him. His legs were wide apart and his mouth was huge. A blaze of triumph shone through his narrow eyes. There in the middle of nowhere was a huge tortoise.

"It's enormous," he said without moving. "We could buy the whole market with what we can get for this."

We hurried back. Near the village he whispered to me: "Listen. Spend tonight in the barn. At dawn when the dogs begin to bark, get up and make haste."

After dinner I yawned and looked at Mother.

"You want to go to bed, son?" she said sweetly. "Go up to your bunk with your sister."

I did not move.

"Didn't you hear what I said?" she said crossly.

I hesitated a moment and tossed a hand grenade into their midst: "I want to sleep in the barn."

"In the barn!" the three of them all shouted. They glared at me as if I had committed some heinous sin.

"Why in the barn, you wretch?" Father said.

My heart beat like a drum at the entry of the bride, and I said quickly: "I want to protect the cattle against robbers."

"You!" Father bawled. "Since when have you been old enough to protect us against robbers? Just get up to your bunk, you turd, and stop all this nonsense."

Bayyah looked at me.

"It's not cattle you're concerned about in the barn," she

33

said. "Wait a moment." She went out and returned. "There's nothing in the barn. But there's something on his mind, I'm certain."

The bitch! Always in my way. I've cursed her many a time. I then quickly got into the bunk so they would not find out my secret.

"There's something on his mind," repeated Bayyah, "and I'm going to find out."

For a long time I tossed and turned, fantasising, my mind full of those delightful stories Ugly Salih had told me. Then I dozed off, I don't know how. When I woke up the dog was barking in great excitement. I so wanted to set eyes on that world of wonders, if only for an hour, and had been planning how to slip out without anybody noticing. I slid to the floor and Bayyah grabbed me from behind.

"Where are you off to, you bastard?"

"I want a pee."

"Do you really want a pee, or is it your secret in the barn?"

Before I could answer, human voices were mingled with the barking of dogs, The din got louder and woke the whole village. When the barking died down I heard sobbing that was like a hungry animal. Then Father's voice thundered: "You dog! What are you doing here?"

"I agreed with him to go to al-'Ala," whimpered Ugly Salih.

Bayyah pushed me towards the door. In the pale dawn light I saw the two of them. Father had a terrified, frail, misshapen, downtrodden Ugly by the scruff of the neck. When father shook him the tortoise fell.

"What's this?" shouted Father.

"A tortoise."

"A tortoise?"

"We were going to sell it at al-'Ala market."

"Sell it at al-'Ala market?"

"Yes."

Father got angrier and beat him and then threw him to one

side as if he were a date stone, and turned to me.

"You want to sell a tortoise? What are people going to say about us when they see you at the market of al-'Ala selling a tortoise?"

Then I was attacked on both sides, Father in front and Bayyah from behind. From a distance Mother egged them on.

"Beat him until the wretch knows right from wrong."

For two days after that I was bound hand and foot. Every hour one of them came to give me my quota of kicks and beatings.

That was my first adventure.

At the age of fourteen I obtained a primary school certificate, and police in a jeep came and told Father I had got first prize. They took me with them to Kairouan.

When I returned I found collections of stories of Kamil al-Kailani and Hans Christian Andersen. Mother wept with delight. Bayyah wept for joy. Father looked at her distantly and then gave me a look and I realised that I had grown up and that none of them would ever beat me again.

One cold February day Father collapsed in a field as he was looking after the cattle. They brought him home and when people gathered round he said: "I want my son."

I was in Kairouan. The telegram arrived in the morning. I was home by noon. He looked at me for a long while.

"Read me something from the book of God, my son," he said.

I read five suras to him: al-Rahman, Yasin, al-Baqara, Yusuf and al-Nisa.

When I finished he took my hand and said: "I can now die in peace."

His eyes then closed for the last time.

*Translated by Peter Clark*

# My Father's Ox

## HASSAN NASR

Poor mother! She's still standing where I left her, waiting for me. Does she think I'm going to be late getting back to her? I haven't wasted a single minute. I crossed the whole distance running, the dust from the road rising to my nose and the sun's sweltering heat scorching my forehead as I became drenched in sweat.

What shall I tell her, now? She'll be angry, most certainly. Yet, is it my fault? It's Uncle Rabih who has caused all the delay. I'm not one to create a delay on purpose.

I found him sick, sitting up in bed. He seemed to be anxious. As soon as he saw me, he clung to me. He asked me about my mother, about my younger brothers, and about the farm: how was it going? Was it still as good as when my father was alive, when he ran it? Was I able to shoulder the responsibilities of the farm after my father's death?

Then he asked me about the ox he had sold to my father a long time ago when he used to deal in cattle and travel to far-off places. He followed this occupation for many years before sickness disabled him. He knew all the kinds of oxen and could distinguish between the different breeds. When an ox was sick, he treated it himself. He knew all the diseases of oxen and the remedy to be used for each.

As he talked to me, I liked this man. I liked him more than I had ever liked anyone else before. I liked the calm way he sat, his swarthy face, his white beard that looked like tufts of cotton on a plantation. His manner of talking made me increasingly fond of him. There was calmness in his speech, there was tenderness, there was a flow like a stream. No one could be bored, even if he spoke for hours on end. When I mentioned to Uncle Rabih that our ox was sick and my mother had sent me to him in the hope that he would help us treat it since we had failed to find a successful remedy ourselves, he was touched and very moved. He wanted to come with me and tried to get up from his bed, but he was too sick and could not manage it. I wished him a full recovery, then left him.

As he ran along the winding narrow path across the fields and saw the figure of his mother in the distance standing in the shade of the tree in front of the farm, Mansur asked himself again: Why is she standing there? The ox must have taken a turn for the worse. Otherwise, she would not have come out in this intense heat to wait for me. I should have come back earlier so that she wouldn't have to face these matters all by herself.

But what use will my arrival be? What can I do for her, or for this ox? Absolutely nothing, except that I will stand there silently and she will stand beside me. And we will continue to watch the ox as it struggles with death, until it finally reaches its end. That is, if my mother chooses to remain quiet and watch how the last curtain falls on the last story of the ox my father bought.

But, if she chooses to go on making up potions for this ox right to the last minute, if she chooses to gather herbs for it and asks me to help her in this endeavour, if she chooses to do that, then I cannot do anything except leave her and turn my face to the fields. That is because I do not want to search for a remedy for this ox. What I want is to look for a way to rid myself of it. I have tried to do this many times but I have clashed with my mother every time. I always found her obstructing my way.

I seized the opportunity of her absence from the fields one day and took the ox to market. Scarcely had I sold it and received payment than I was surprised to see my mother. I was caught unaware as, in front of all the people, she landed blow upon blow on me. I was forced to hand over to her what I had received and leave the market.

My mother is a stern and strong woman and I was afraid of her. And I was unable to do anything because, quite simply, she could prevent me. So I tried to explain things to her differently. I said to her: "Instead of the ox, I want to buy an engine like the one our neighbour Mabruk bought. Such an engine can, in a short time, easily pump the water for us from the depths of the well, and in greater abundance than bucketfuls."

At this point I did not stop. I even took her with me to our neighbour's field and she saw how water was gushing along the irrigation canals and how two workers were diverting it into the ditches but were overwhelmed by its force. My mother liked the scene of the large pool that looked like a lake, as the water poured into it from the well without the help of an ox, or a bucket, or even a human being.

What happened was that, after we returned to our field, she said to me: "My son, before he died your father advised me to keep this ox and not allow it to be taken from us at any price. The loss of it would be a loss both to us and to our field. And, furthermore, even if there is something that could take the place of the ox in bringing up the water from the well, I don't think there is anything that can take its place in ploughing the earth. It is better for us, my son, to keep this ox that your father bought from his hard work and the sweat of his brow. We must not allow it to be taken from us, whatever the cost. We are not in need of more water. Our bucket, which the ox carries for us, is sufficient and even more than sufficient."

I could not tolerate such words, so on that day I left the house in case I did something that my mother would not like or that would harm her. Was it true that the amount of water carried for us in the bucket was sufficient? How about the rest of the farm? Would we leave it to go thirsty until its greenness died? How about the labour, the sweat? Would all that be in vain?

Why should it always be this ox at the centre of things?

I am sick to death of its story. I am sick of the whining of those pulleys that never stops all day long, sick of that movement up and down in the ditch, sick of the ox there in front of me, sick of the ropes before my eyes stretched taut between the ox and the bucket while I am drenched in sweat.

Why does my mother want me to follow the example of my father in everything? To be like him in everything? If my father followed the example of his father in all the things he found him doing in his time, I cannot follow the example of my father in all that he left for me. I cannot live the life of my father. I have my own life, and I live it as it is destined for me. No human being should impose his opinions on me, whatever he might be and whoever he might be. Even if he is my father.


Mansur reached the field and crossed the narrow path leading to the house. He did not turn to his mother but he heard her calling him: "Mansur, what is the matter with you, my son? Why are you so late?"

"It's not me who wanted that. It's the man you sent me to see. He's the reason I've been delayed all this time!"

"And where is he now? Why has he not come with you?"

"I found that he is sick."

"Did you tell him how the ox was?"

"Yes, I told him. He wanted to come with me, but he was too sick and could not even get up from his bed."

The mother bowed her head for a long time, thinking. Then she turned to her son and said, in a voice that was like sorrow itself, "And have you thought about the ox?"

Mansur wanted to keep silent and not answer the question

but rather continue on his way. However, he took hold of himself and said to his mother: "Thinking is no longer my concern from now on."

"Whose concern is it, then?"

"It is your concern."

"It is my concern! And how is that?"

Mansur could not add a single word. He turned his eyes to the fields. He then walked to where he had left the ox in the shade of the vine.

There, he found it lying on its side, its great black head wrenched backwards, its forelegs thrusting forwards, its thick tail lying flattened beneath its body as if it were not part of it. Flies were gathering around its nose, near its eyes and on different parts of its body.

This enormous body, spread out under the full shade of the vine, looked as if it had been dead for a long while. Mansur looking at it silently and his mother came up and stood beside him looking at it too. They both saw the ox, little by little, raise its head from the ground. They heard it utter a great deep moo that echoed over the distant fields. It moved its forelegs and twitched, and it mooed a second time. Then its head fell back on to the ground and it was no longer a living thing.

*Translated by Issa J Boullata*

# Wind

## ALI MOSBAH

Here, one can see the wind.

Between the mountains of Zaghouan in the west and
Fkirine in the east, there is a corridor that is neither part of
the northern plains, nor part of the slopes below. Mere hills
scattered between the two mountains and positioned to set off
the fertile northern sector, where wheat is as tall as men, from
the barren lands of the middle, bursting with jagged stones
and useless prickly shrubs. The wind blows through this pas-
sageway from the end of autumn to the beginning of summer
and its howl morphs from sobbing, to wailing, to the maddening trumpet blows of demons and genies.

A howling wind, indeed.

Bringing blistering, depressing cold, or scorching southern
heat; the desirable mandara wind that winnows grain from
the ears of corn, or the flirting wind that takes away the laun-
dry or upturns women's skirts. The wind of laziness and disease and death. The wind that steers the feet of dervishes and
the sails of eternal travellers, and snatches people away and
never brings them back.

The southern wind of late spring and early summer, brim-
ming with the desert dryness that ripens peppers and tomatoes, but that might also bring locusts and scorpions and
pythons and lice and the plague and trachoma. It cooks up
the Indian cactus and fans the instincts of the he-goat, but
might make women barren, as old women say.

And the northern mountain wind that shrouds the world with sadness as it whistles over the roofs and among the trees, twisting cypresses and willow trees, and mildly swaying the heavy, round olive trees. The smaller olive trees are easier victims, and their broken branches often prompt the saddened farmers to appeal to God for more compassion. Sometimes, my father gathers the fallen branches and drags them home with the deep misery of a soldier carrying the bodies of fallen comrades.

My mother quarrels with the wind and curses it, and occasionally curses people I don't know, which makes me wonder about their connection to the wind. She looks at that invisible being, reproaches it or swears at it, and then shouts at me: "Come on in, chick, before the wind shakes you up," and I do go in but she never gives a full accounting of all those people she curses. When she lines up the broken branches, she talks to them, relating their previous bounties, and lamenting their current destiny as firewood for the clay bread oven, the tannour.

A rather touching sight is that of slender cypress trees that bend and swing with the wind like a group of wailing women. Their delicate branches defy the carnage, never surrendering to the wind, and leaning one against the other.

When the cold February wind blows, outside doors are locked and people venture out only for emergencies. Chickens find refuge in reed sheds, forever pecking the ground and never relinquishing their safe haven. They might be surprised once in a while by a dog that cannot settle in a hay stack or a cosy corner in the stable, or simply because it is bored and wants to move around.

Among the olive trees, stray donkeys look as if they could not care less for the wind, or for anything else. They do not feed or seek shelter but stay out there like discarded things in the wilderness. Donkeys are strange; how utterly trivial and useless they look in the midst of a howling wind! Just black spots marking a dull space or final touches dotting the landscape of misery that the wind brings to the scene. Sheep could not care less, either. They keep on grazing regardless under that protective ball of wool. No wind will shake them, their limbs are tougher than the branches of peach and pomegranate trees and no wind will ruin their appetite. Goats are cowardly, or too finicky and selfish and have little inclination to bond with their like. They disperse like hay and dust in the face of the wind as if the wind were a pack of wolves. Goats bond only when it rains.

*Iron cast is the roof of my home*
*Its corners solid stone*
*Let the wind howl!*
*Let the rain pour!*

Throngs of school children swarm along the winding dirt road between rows of olive trees. Human mass are nudged in the back like tiny balls by the wind. Their loud, merry voices defy the wind, come from the depths of the woods and reverberate in the distance. Some scatter in the wind, others carry flashes of joy and song in their faces. Just before the evening, the children will be heading in the opposite direction, against the wind. Their small bodies will bend, their thin legs will buckle, struggling to keep their balance. On such a day, they will not stop to finish the game of marbles they started at midday in the school yard, or watch a couple of mates settling an argument with hands and legs, or cluster to work together on a maths or language exercise. They'll continue chanting their school songs as they chew on the remains of the bread they brought in the morning for their lunch. Now, it is covered with chalk and ink stains, but remains the most delicious snack even though mothers try to make their supper more nourishing, with hot stew and vegetables, and even a chunk of meat if God happens to bless a deal or if a goat is sick or happens to fall from the roof. High winds have their benefits, too.

*Iron cast is the roof of my home*
*Its corners solid stone*
*Let the wind howl!*
. . .

On such a day they won't chant this chorus with enthusiasm. Words stick in the throat on a windy day. This is real
wind, not the wind in a chant, and they can see it breaking
the branches of the majestic eucalyptus tree in the school
yard, bending men's bodies, and ballooning their woollen
kashabiyas till they appear to fly, or trot like airmen the
moment they touch the ground. The wind can untie an old
man's waistband and toss his kashabiya over his head like a
kite, and the poor fellow will falter as he pursues the flying
garment, seeking refuge in God from the workings of Satan.
A wind bold enough to lift up a woman's dress or abaya and
expose her thighs to the looks of men and boys. Some will
turn away, out of modesty or consideration for the victim;
others will stare with eyes wide open as the woman bats the
dress down with both hands in rapid, clumsy movements.
The young get a kick out of such a flash of exposed flesh, the
flash of light from the thunder on a pitch-black night.

No house has an iron-cast roof. The better-off who own
the estates left by the last colonials live in villas finished off by
red bricks. The rest live in mud huts whose roofs are made
from hay and branches of willow and pine trees. It's a little
peculiar, perhaps even foolhardy, to brag about such roofs in
the face of winds and storms. Children have often seen roofs
ripped off by storms and turned into loose hay and weeds,
blown away alongside kitchen utensils, old floor mats, blan-
kets and clothes. And the villas are not necessarily safer since
many have not been maintained for years. The bricks lining
their roofs do not last in the face of stormy winds and the
children often curse Nuiama and their own artlessness for
believing the empty words of a poet who doesn't know what

44

he's talking about. Their doubts might even extend to all school books and the vague stuff in them that seem drawn from fables and myths.

The storm might last for one day, three, or seven days, but rarely for two, four, or five days. The one-day trick is acceptable and the three-day is just a rainy storm. But the seven-day is an ordeal. It is also called the afreet storm because the fifth day brings the anxious wait for the sandstorm that cloaks the afreet, who is shackled in gold chains, as old women claim. These are the chains the Almighty ordained to keep the destructive creature from wrecking the entire world.

"But where is the afreet going to?"

"To prison. God transfers it from one jail to another wrapped in a sandstorm, for the protection of the world."

"And God lifts it with the storm to its remote prison?"

"The storm is the mighty breath of that creature, heralding a presence surrounded with dust and hay and thorns."

"But why doesn't God leave it in a permanent prison in one corner of the world since it brings all these catastrophes?"

We will not get an answer for that question but our consolation is the day off we get on the day the afreet is expected to pass. It's not only a break from school, but also from gathering firewood and shepherding. We stay indoors around the stove and listen to old women's stories about someone who actually saw the afreet with his own eyes. A strange creature, he said, that looked like a python the size of a willow tree with a heavy chain of pure gold around its massive, hairy neck. He would have stolen the gold chain but for an unexpected turn of events. And stories of a woman who insisted on getting firewood during the afreet sandstorm, only to be carried away by the storm, and to date never heard of again. And a man who was blown away by the wind as he tried to lay stones and iron bars on a hay stack, and was thrown with a bundle of hay and dust for at least a hundred metres.

The one-week storm also brings death. Once, ten lives were snuffed out in that week of horror. Its howl over the roofs was echoed by the wailing that rose from the rest of the village. Grief scorched people's faces and bent their bodies, twisted the tops of trees, and paralysed roads and fields. An odd mixture of silence and moaning fit only for the face of death. Silence in the shops and assemblies of men, and in the processions to and from the cemetery, and wailing and weeping elsewhere that the wind broke down and subsumed in its own roar.

It was on the sandstorm day of such an ordeal that German troops landed one distant year, and on the eve of such a day that the daughter of the village Mukhtar eloped with a Bedouin. He used to sing at weddings and completely bewitched her. The Mukhtar stayed away from men's gatherings until his death from a broken heart. And it was on the eve of a sandstorm that the sergeant surprised his wife, his junior by twenty years, groaning in the stable with one of his shepherds. "The bitch never groaned like this with me!" He did no't hesitate to pull the trigger and soon after was locked away in a remote prison. And once, the sandstorm brought a disease that killed all the livestock, sparing only donkeys and mules.


On a stifling summer day people need a little wind, a delicate breeze that separates grains from the chaff after threshing. This is the mandara breeze we wait for in the early evening, and when it fails to come, the air dries up and threshers have to fall back on tricks to winnow the grain from the ears. They ask the kids to lie.

Lying draws the wind, and that's why we couple liars with the wind. A strange connection as if the wind blows solely to scatter lies. Perhaps winds are types of discourse we don't understand, and what's lying, when you think of it, but loose talk that is like windy discourse. We loved that trick and competed to show our ingenuity in lying to tempt the wind. We told of sleeping pythons we stumbled on in the valley, a cow wearing glasses and reading a heavy book, and the teacher with the fearful cane entering the classroom with the head of a calf. And of a lark we trapped and were about to slaughter but which then appealed to us in formal Arabic to let it go to feed its nestlings.

Adults enjoyed our lies and made us feel important, but the wind rarely rewarded us. Somebody would say: "These are bare-faced lies that will not bring wind", and advise us to come up with more credible ones.

The oppressively hot weather persists, and it feels like the entire universe is trapped inside an oven. Still trees with branches like stone; threshers monotonously beating ears of wheat; and tired men half-heartedly whipping their tired horses. The water-wheel at the well stops, and people stare at the stony branches of willow and fig and olive trees.

The only thing that could spark some life was the transistor radio. That tiny box, which drew people away from their habitual gatherings and their master storytellers, became the centre piece in a home, or in the open field when people were working.The radio reduced grandmothers to silence, or sometimes to death, and turned screaming kids into dutiful listeners. Some thought the talk coming out of that box was worthless lies and they even used radios to trick the wind. It was a windy day when the first radio came to the village.

Ahmed El-Nuri put the radio on a stack of wheat stalks tied tightly together. He fiddled with its buttons and ariel, and shouted"Yes, there it is!"and signalled to his sons and labourers to carry on threshing. El-Nuri wasn't looking for a particular station, he just wanted to get a clear sound out of the set to draw the wind to the area. The chaff was falling to the ground with the grains and the tired workers felt helpless as they looked at the immobile almond and olive trees on the nearby hills. A dog crawled from under a pile of stalks, arched its back and padded slowly toward the house.

Then the men saw the northern horizon getting darker, and the sky becoming the colour of lead when mixed with dirt. The sky turned red, and El-Nuri appealed to God for help. The men muttered a little as they tried to catch their breath. Their bodies were dripping with warm sweat.

Bits of chaff started to separate from the grains and El-Nuri declared: "The wind is blowing." The rhythm of the beating flails intensified and at the top of the willow the leaves quivered a little. Chickens started to move towards the cow byre.

"It's a sandstorm," El-Nuri shouted. "You sons of bitches, cover the pile of wheat and lay heavy stones on top of it. Covers. Plastic mats. And stones," he cried and ran around in a frenzy. The men stopped threshing and ran for the plastic covers. Chaff started to waft away from the wheat and cover the left side of the threshing area in a delicate white bloom.

It was the middle of summer and we thought we were safe from sandstorms and their afreets. What was Ahmed El-Nuri thinking when he fiddled with the radio? Perhaps he just missed the breeze he wanted and so messed up the sequence of seasons inside that astonishing box. Anyway, when the men finally got the plastic covers and started securing them over the wheat, they could barely keep standing. It became dark even though there was not a single cloud in the sky. Soon after, firewood, empty cartons, sheets of paper, utensils and items of clothing were blowing all over the place. The workers had no time to lay large stones over the covers and Ahmed El-Nuri continued to curse them. They had to sit on the covers to keep them in place, especially after the wind scattered a big pile of firewood.

"Sit on it and hold on to the covers with your hands and teeth, you sons of bitches," El-Nuri bewailed and hit the ground with his stick. "You'll bankrupt me . . ." and his angry explosion of orders and curses came to a stop when he saw the stack of wheat on which he had put his radio fly into the air taking the set with it. His djellaba was filled with air as he bent to pick something up, then it lifted right up. It appeared he didn't have anything under that djellaba and people turned away, struggling to smother their laughter. His sons couldn't look either, at that sudden exposure of the patriarch. The wind twisted him around when he struggled to right his clothing and after a few seconds his hand disappeared as the wind took the garment. Another section of the pile soon followed and the men had to flee when one of them was blown away along with the mat he was sitting on. The sandstorm then took hold of the entire place, spinning the ears of wheat and chaff and grain, the mats and plastic covers and sheets of paper into the air, accompanied by the last curses Ahmed El-Nuri uttered. El-Nuri and the man on the flying mat became completely invisible.

For the children, nothing could have been more entertaining than the exposed nakedness of a grown-up cursing, and the sudden collapse of his formidable authority. They might even wish under such circumstances that the sandstorm would whisk them away a few metres over the houses and fields, just to scare their parents a little, so that in those scary moments they would regret their harsh treatment of the children. The children also imagined that after they survived the stormy adventure, they would return home victorious, to crying and remorseful parents ready to abandon cruel ways with them. But the firm hands of adults did not let them join the storm, so the children confined themselves to joyous and loud shouts to celebrate the grown-ups' ludicrous loss of control. Children could not care less for what the wind blew away. If anything, they might have envied Ahmed El-Nuri for his ride to one of the remote places of their imagination, regardless of their hilarious reaction to his exposed behind.

Ahmed El-Nuri was found shortly after the storm. Some heard his helpless moans in a thicket and they soon stumbled on him, his djellaba still around his head, his body stark naked. He fell sick and could not or would not eat or speak for more than two weeks, but he acquired the ability to sense an approaching wind or storm and could tell with unbelievable accuracy its type and direction and when it would be arriving and ending. No one found the radio, however. Old and young failed to find even a screw, no matter how hard they searched. Some thought it was possessed by a wind djinn and others said it was a mere receptacle of lies that the wind had come to take to wherever it should. Anyway, no other radio was allowed into the village, and adults had to fall back on children's lies to tempt the wind during the threshing season. Or until the mechanical harvesters arrived that put an end to the threshing floor and all its gear.

No mechanical device has been invented yet to stop a wind or storm. They continue to blow between mountain Zaghouan and mountain Fkirine but without the caravan of summer labourers heading towards the northern plains for the harvest season. And the caravan heading south towards Kairouan and Sidi Bou Said, loaded with men and women singing to the tunes of their clanking utensils. Also gone are the inscrutable, suspicious travellers wrapped, summer and winter, in their woollen kashabiyas and dark hoods, with nothing but their bright eyes to be seen. They slept where they could during the day and at night they bewitched women and horses with their singing. And gone are the palm readers and the itinerant sellers riding pitiable donkeys. And the beggars whose chants were scattered by the wind with what remained of them sounding more like notes of an arcane puzzle.

Only the wind continues to move between Zaghouan in the east and Fkirine in the west and but for the olives and the eucalyptus and the cypresses and the almond trees one would never know it was there.

*Translated by Shakir Mustafa*

# *Hulagu*

## MUHAMMAD MUSTAGAB

In the year nineteen twenty and something, leaving the city of Qus behind him, my grandfather headed out with companions on a journey to the heart of the Eastern desert mountains. As the sun set on the eve of the fifth day, the one road they were taking became ten, eyes became unfocused, camels frothed and breaths quickened. That was when my grandfather whispered to the companion nearest to him: "We're lost." The companion, unable to control himself, began blubbering in an embarrassing fashion — his sobs became contagious, and soon everyone was slapping their hands desperate to know what to do next. They spent hours beseeching Almighty God to guide them to a good road as they were on their way to visit His sacred house and the grave of the good Prophet.

During the following five frightful days, as the men became exhausted and their spirits deflated, as the camels weakened and any hope of the pilgrimage was shattered, all hearts had only one hope, to find a road to anywhere. But my grandfather was strong and he made an oath, in secret, that should he be delivered from this predicament, he would build for God a mosque unequalled in the village. A few hours later, he and his friends found themselves on the edges of the city of Qus. Bastards, as well as those who do not wish our family well, say that my grandfather was the reason why this happened; that standing by the Black stone would have been his unique chance to ask for God's help against his rivals; but his attempt

51

to make the hajj was insincere, resulting in God siding with the enemies. One of them even slaughtered a sheep the day my grandfather returned from the pilgrimage without a hajj.

One thing certain was that the next morning my grandfather started his initiative on his own. He walked around the village for a long time, then stood at the edge of a muddy triangular hole created by a stream at the entrance to the village. Squatting down, he measured the area carefully, drawing logarithmic lines, then stood up, threw his woollen hajj shawl back over his shoulders and recited the first chapter of the Qur'an, signalling the carrying out of his secret vow to build a mosque the like of which the village had never seen.

At a gathering permeated with religious entreaty, my grandfather sat surrounded by his sons and his supporters. There was wheat in the granaries, sugar cane in the factories and sheep in the fields – so, was there any particular objection? No one said a word. They left the meeting feeling closer to God than at any other time before.

In one month, the muddy hole was no more and the building had reached about a metre high. Construction then stopped due to a very ordinary event: one day my aunt went to wake my grandfather and found he had given up the ghost.

Sometimes in a situation like this God would provide a man with a strong personality who could rally others around him to complete what a great man had started, one who hadn't had the chance of proving the sincerity of his intentions or disproving his rivals and enemies. Considering that such a man did not exist in my family, the one-metre structure remained neglected in its narrow triangle, water accumulating in its pit.

With the religious inclination of dogs being questionable, during the following winter some passed by the low walls and raised their hind legs to water the weeds that had sprung up between the stones. It wasn't long before there were lizards, stagnant water and hornets' nests, giving the place an atmosphere to frighten the faint-hearted.

I have an uncle who was facing troubles: he had broken his right leg trying to climb over the wall of a widow with a good measure of beauty – on a mission whose details I'm not aware of. For a while the man remained a burden on his brothers. When he sensed they were getting tired of him, he borrowed some money – probably from the same widow – and bought some crates which he arranged and filled with tomatoes, cucumbers, string beans, and tangerines. Alert and energetic, he received his customers in the early morning. It wasn't long before news of his important commercial enterprise reached the edges of the village, whereupon his brothers and the rest of the family rose to defend an honour that was about to be sullied – within the area of the unfinished structure of the mosque. Emergency fatwas were issued by groups of other families that proved, without a shadow of doubt, that the use of a mosque (despite it being incomplete, and however many times one tried to clean it up) for the business of buying and selling was the very core of unbelief and that it was better to tear down what had been built of the mosque rather than have some good-for-nothing practise such a disgraceful act during the hours of day (no mention, of course, of what could happen in the same place at night).

The logical conclusion was that the mosque had to be completed. Other families joined us in that position. One grandee of the family raised his palm in a gesture of objection: after all the matter did not concern us alone. The family sold some distant land that did not bring much profit (by the way, there were those who questioned the reason God provided for our grandfather and why those blessings had not spread to include the rest of the family) and started work on the building. It rose another few metres – the mosque beginning to take form – until it reached neck-height, at which time the village was stormed by a group of building inspectors.

Who is responsible for this building here? My strong middle uncle – one without a limp – stepped forward as if about to receive an achievement award. "I am." The powers that be took away my prodigious uncle at the beginning of 1937, abandoning him to a prison sentence of two months with hard labour for erecting public buildings without consulting the authorities and without obtaining a special permit. The village placed its hand over its mouth in wonder, in bewilderment, irritation, sarcasm and even modesty. One thing certain was that construction stopped, and the dogs, hornets, and smelly water reappeared, as well as bats whose activities outdid all the other elements combined.

My eldest brother was a man in the full meaning of the masculine term. He was unlike my grandfather or any of my paternal uncles. He had received a school diploma and his uncles managed to get him a job in the governorate of Asyut. He lived away from us and had become a major resource for all the villagers: whoever had a case in Asyut, a man called up for military service or someone wanting to bribe the water inspector, or anyone who wanted to invest the small sum he'd made from cotton, would pass by my brother and he would attend to their requests until their missions were completed.

My brother became famous, more so than 'Abd al-'Alim, the village headman, and Ahmad Khamis, the poet. The idea of building the mosque was not far from my brother's mind as he fathomed out discussions in the governorate on the importance of building schools in rural areas for the education of the masses (of course).

My brother wasn't stupid. He came to the village and reviewed the matter with his brothers. He stressed that the village was not so much in need of a mosque as it was in need of a school; that the village had thirteen mosques and several Sufi retreats, while its only school was part of an old mosque, and subsidised by grain and Egyptian bread, and run by Sheikh 'Abd al-Wadud who unfortunately belonged to one of the rival families. Besides, with education coming straight after prayer in God's eyes, one could also earn a lot of money. They would own a school staffed by teachers, a headmaster and inspectors, and receive a respectable monthly rent, so: "Hand me the power of attorney!" My brother received that power of attorney. He sold some land and got a building permit. He roofed the school and expanded it by buying additional land. He divided the building into two floors, the floors into rooms; he rubbed his hands contentedly and went out to have a second look at the building. Then he walked to the train station to finish matters in Asyut. On the other side of the road he noticed some Bedouins hammering pegs into the ground. "What's up, boys?"

"We're landscapers measuring out for the new school."

A man with a hard hat came out and greeted him, saying: "We're in a rush. We have to hand over to the contractor by tomorrow so he can complete the building before next winter."

My brother collapsed and died. He was buried in April 1950.

My name is such-and-such. I graduated two years ago from the Liberal Arts College. I do some light work, like giving private lessons, as I wait to be appointed. I met – during a hitch-hiking tour of Europe – some French people whom I invited to visit our village, and they came. Among them was Marianna, a beautiful and talkative woman who enjoys special individual qualities, such as the ability to grab hold of anything from anywhere.

Marianna took in the building, consuming it with her green eyes; then screamed with delight at how fabulous it was. She was ready to invest all she owned in a rest house for tourists coming and going to Luxor and Aswan. Her ideas were modern and clear. The building was wonderful. The main road that passed through Upper Egypt was a stone's throw from where we were. Marianna wanted to bring over her sister, a dancer in cheap night clubs, to add warmth to the place. Her words were logical and comforting.

*Translated by Mona Zaki*

# Sardines and Oranges

## MOHAMMED ZEFZAF

The mouth of the river is very strange. At one time its water reflected the blue sky. Now the colour is murky and filthy like mud. Lots of factories were built on its bank. These factories are not interesting apart for two, which can oranges and sardines.

The canning factories have two huge craters, dumps for rotten oranges and sardines. Further along, about five kilometers away, there is another large crater for the garbage of the French naval base. The best bits of refuse are wet bread, jars of unfinished jams or fruits, soggy biscuits and other stuff that might be prohibited for Muslims to eat. But we eat it anyway, since Independence gave us back the land but not food. First, the French left behind their crater for us to pick through. Then two more craters were added: one for rotten oranges and the other for rotten sardines. Nature gave us an oak forest. Unwatched, we collect bags of nuts, or, close to a stream, we hunt birds that we roast or sell. Most of the time we do not roast them – they are thin, hungry birds not even the size of small pigeons. Anyone could eat the whole bird in one mouthful: bones and all. You see, the bay is very strange. About twelve kilometers upstream another base was set up. Unfortunately, the French throw in things we do not recognise, some sink to the bottom of the river and the rest drift off to the Atlantic ocean. We don't know where these glittering, dark, big or small objects go. One thing for sure is that it isn't food, otherwise we would see the fish jumping over the ocean surface, that is, if the fish in the river have left anything. By the way, ocean fish are beautiful and lively, gleaming under the sun as they jump in the air. River fish are heavy, dark and easily caught in the nets of small boats. Any human should be excused from eating those. That is why they sell them to towns far from the rivers and the ocean and the Mediterranean. How beautiful the lively fish from the ocean are!

Once we stole a box of fish from near one of the small boats on the marina by the bay. Some were large, others small but they weren't lively because they were dead! We never tasted anything like them before. Only Europeans eat these fish as they are expensive. I suspect that ocean fish are not intended for our mouths. But we liked the taste. We hastily hid the box under a bushy tree. We saw the owner, who could have been a trader in the central market for Europeans and other Moroccans, wail and slap his face and thighs. "The food for my children is gone!" he screamed. We saw him running round in circles. He went to the auction site and picked out a man wearing waders. They got into a fist fight and the owner said: "I swear by God I won't leave you till I kill you! You've taken the food out of my children's mouths, you son of a bitch!"

We hid and we don't know if he killed him or not. But the ocean fish tasted delicious. I never tasted anything like that in my life before. Not even my mother knew how to prepare it – whether to grill it, or fry it, or bake it. I don't know what the mothers of the other three that we split the box with did. Except for that one feast, what we scavenge barely fills our bellies. The nuts we eat fried or boiled. We eat so many of them when they're in season that we get sick and throw up. There were many other feasts we enjoyed but not that year.

Locusts filled the skies. The bigger ones among us would collect bags of locusts and sell them grilled outside schools and local cinemas. Europeans do not eat locusts. We can't understand why, when they eat pigs, frogs, other animals such as cats or dogs, and other creatures we would spot on their plates in restaurants. People eat what they want to eat. Some choose water melons, some choose beef or radishes. But the fish from the ocean are the best despite being so pricey and even though they fly on top of the water. Because they are hard to catch, large fishing vessels come from far-away countries. It is a pity we don't have big vessels to catch those beautiful lively fish. Even if we didn't eat them, we could put them in bowls of water and gaze at them longingly.

I always think Independence gave us the land (or gave some people land, I don't know) but not the sea. Sometimes I see short people who have narrow eyes and are different in colour. They seem kind and speak another language. They catch these beautiful lively fish, then go and drink something in the coffee shops and take fish like the ones we caught in the box and did not know how to cook. But we all know how to cook the sardines and the river snakes. Sometimes these river snakes can be poisonous just like land snakes. I didn't know this and haven't seen them. I was told about it by somebody. I also heard about people in other countries who eat land snakes. We eat the river snakes.

Anyway, this world is strange, just like the mouth of the river. Some people have narrow eyes, others have black skin, some blond hair. Some have seas they don't know how to fish from. And there are those who have gained Independence just like us and are given two craters, one for rotten sardines and the other for rotten oranges they cannot export or preserve. There is also the third crater with the refuse from the French naval base. I don't know if other nations who gained their Independence have as many craters; I also don't know if they have seas like the Atlantic Ocean with fish flying over the surface and its people unable to catch them. Do you have other people come over and catch beautiful lively fish? Do they know how to cook them?

At any rate, we gained our Independence and the land is

ours. And we also have ministers who are Moroccan. I heard one of them one day give a speech. He was a brilliant man and I stood in the centre of a dusty arena. He said he intended to pull down the shanties we live in and build homes with toilets and a window for sunlight. He didn't come back after that day, nor did he pull down the shanties or build new houses. It's good that he didn't fill up these craters because they're full of flies. He spoke about cleanliness and putting an end to the flies, and my guess is that he didn't know about the three craters overcrowded with humans and flies.

Humans pick through those craters heedless of the flies, which do not bother us at all. Like us, they scavenge the dumps, descending on rotten sardines unfit for export. The flies, like us, want to live. These rotten sardines never hurt my belly and I don't know why they throw them away. Maybe the intestines of those who import the sardines and oranges are weak because they gained their Independence long before us. Maybe they don't have oceans or gardens, or their seas and rivers have dried up and their stomachs are not used to digesting these sardines. All this is to our benefit. Let the rivers and seas dry up or their intestines disintegrate so that we can be left undisturbed with what we find. It appears that their intestines are able to digest those delicious, beautiful, lively fish and other things in the sea that have horns, claws, tails, wings, beaks and nails. And I believe that if we eat any of those things we would get bellyache, diarrhoea or something.

Even in Morocco we have people, like those foreigners, who cannot digest anything, even things like mutton, beef or rabbit. One of the boys who split the box of beautiful lively fish told me that he worked in the home of one of those rich Moroccans, who would have parties with roast lamb, chicken and lots of fruit and fish. But the man could not eat and would have a bowl of soup without any spices. He explained that it was because of his illicit food. Oh, my God! How much better it is that a person can eat rotten sardines and oranges from a hole in the ground than to have an illicit gut!

All consumers of unlawful food are rejected among the living first and then by God. I think if they ate from our crater it would be better for them. They might become stronger and not catch any diseases. As for us, we never get indigestion. Sometimes we get eye-sores, rashes or yellow fever because we swim in the swamp. That is what my mother said and she beat me often because of that. When I did catch the yellow fever, or the blue or other fevers that I do not know the colour of, my mother would beat me and tell me not to go to the swamp again with so-and-so. That is not important. She would not beat me when we went to the dump and filled our pockets or rusty boxes with rotten sardines; or when we carried rotten oranges in plastic bags or what looked like plastic bags that I can't remember how we got hold of. Details don't matter, the oranges would reach the house or be sold on the street. Everyone needs to eat, whether in the home or the street. Anyone who could not eat those things would have to roast lamb or drink soup without spices and his belly would swell up with the illicit food.

But I still don't know how illicit food can make bellies big. We eat a lot of oranges, sardines, nuts and our bellies don't get big. We also eat a lot of other things. We grow tall, our bodies thin out but our bellies don't get bigger. It seems to me that the difference between halal and haram is between eating from the crater outside the canning factory – this is better for you – and eating what they produce inside. Those who eat the canned food from the factories have enlarged bellies and those who eat from the outside craters grow taller with higher foreheads and shrunken stomachs. It is the right of every human to eat. We were created so we can eat our fill from the goodness of this world.

I know that when we die we will eat grapes, pomegranates, honey and the white bread the French eat in restaurants. I tasted it once and placed a piece in between the wheat bread my mother bakes every day. Because man is created to eat and feel full we decided one day to return to the small marina to steal another box of the delicious, beautiful lively fish. One of us said he feared we would get caught and sent to prison. We know that in prison there are a lot of lice — this has been reported to us by some who came out. Are prison lice larger than the lice outside prison, ones that stick to our shorts? Often we would go near the railway tracks, take our shorts off and remove the lice. Lice are the same: in or out of prison. That is why we don't worry about prison. We walked that morning to the marina to steal another box of those delicious, beautiful lively fish. Man was born to eat and feel full.

*Translated by Mona Zaki*

# The Myth of the North

## IZZ AL-DIN AL-TAZI

Here I am; I stopped for a while amazed by all that I see; a world as bright and violent as the refrain I woke up repeating to myself. I found myself dancing, crying, then falling into reflection not knowing what had become of me. I woke up remembering my strange clothes, my features not reflected in mirrors and everything else surrounding me all blending into a carnival of sounds and movements of various meanings. Did I stop? I may have stopped walking on the unpaved sand road. The rain, the little wetness settled the turbulent sands despite continuous stormy winds.

I have probably forgotten the refrain by now. From here I can see the sea and the cemeteries and my footsteps that have crossed this road time and again without noticing all these things I now clearly see. I opened my misty eyes and saw myself stopping and it occurred to me that I could not continue walking because I felt tired. I did not think of stopping but I did; and when I did I tried to find out why. My tiredness explained it as well as the weight of the vegetables and the fruits I was carrying in my hands.

> *The sea and the graves*
> *lote and cactus trees*
> *the dusty land*
> *perforated domes, rundown tombstones and the eyes of owls.*

Behind all this the sea extends with piercing brightness like the edge of a sword. Its seductive blue dissipates the surrounding desolation. I never saw a ship or a boat scratch that clean blue surface. I never felt the presence of the sea, its blue murky with the black. The sea never occurred to me to be some superfluous addition; it meant nothing as long as it did not carry any meaning. I laughed at the idea of drowning, fishing and swimming: I'm laughing at all this now. Even the thought of complaining, reflecting on it or expressing it seems funny as I now laugh loud enough for the sea to hear me.

On the other side of the road cars and foreign trucks drive by filled with cargo. This is a busy road carrying goods to Africa. The drivers of these large trucks throw out their empty beer bottles and you can spot their fat faces the instant the trucks go by. I remained standing so I could rest holding the vegetables and the fruit. When will I reach the plateau and open the door and finally sink in a chair so I can catch my panting breath?

Here I am! I forgot the face of the doctor and other things that happened after he left. When I came from the south I could not have imagined that the north had so much abundance and joy in everything. The sun that I saw was not the same, nor were the cafés. So many dialects and people celebrating trees, roses and tears. Men cried and so did women with heaving breasts, blushing cheeks and vaporous tears rolling down. Shaving razors, scratches on the cheeks and foreheads. Even children had these scratches on their faces. Knives, killing, foreign currency, guns. I could not go back. The north is the road of no return. I did not write letters. I forgot my family; I sent them nothing from the north. Their names, their features got lost with the years and so did their voices, their movements and gestures. I did not have a family in the north. I was afraid that someone would love me, a man or woman or friend I would have to be faithful to or a woman I would have to become close to and then marry and have children in this north, when in the south I did not have a woman or any children.

The love of the people of the north is lethal. Why should I look for love when people here can kill someone just because they love him? They kill, they commit suicide or they laugh maniacally for the rest of their lives. All the men and women in the north do that; I have seen it. I once saw a child in the north gaze amorously at another in front of a café while the other one avoided him. Onlookers watched without amazement; he then pulled a knife and stabbed him in the heart. I saw an old woman coming out of one of the homes with bloody hands, crying and stupidly telling people "I killed her" as if, when she intended to kill, she had not known what it was she was doing. I saw more than that. I once saw fools standing in front of cafés, each with a story of how he killed someone he loved: a woman, a friend, a son, a lover. The doctor asserted this to me when he was talking about his permanent bachelorhood and his avoidance of people: "It would be better for them to hate me and describe me as unfriendly or a recluse than if they were to love and kill me." He told me: "We cannot speak of death here in the north. It is rare that someone dies. People don't die, they get killed. Every dead person has to die killed." I begged, like the doctor, so I could live and so no one would kill me. My hair greyed, here is my greying moustache, and the wrinkles. No one killed me and now I stand, resting a bit before I continue walking. I learnt Spanish and I helped the doctor attend to Spanish soldiers. I informed on some runaway landlords to the north and here I am, I did not get killed. I drank alone, I slept alone. I ran away from love so that no one would kill me, I closed all the windows and I only saw the frame of the mirror.

Panting breaths

Rapid heart beats

I climbed the uphill road that was full of holes and stones, its sand dampened by last night's rain. They said they were waiting for one of those official visits to get it paved.

The wide fields are visible from the plateau as it extends to the other side. I smell the sea, the earth, they both flow into

64

my soul and make me feel happier and ready for love. Love for what? A man? A woman? For the image or a memory or a reflection? For the love of the family that I have forgotten in the south? The love of God? The love of loneliness, the drink and the sounds of the sea reaching me? For a young girl I saw in a dream? The love of life, of apricots – the large and juicy ones especially, dripping sweetness after a bite or two? The love of song and the voice of Mohammad Abdel Wahab singing "When the evening falls /and the comfort of the night"? The love of my mother; I no longer remember her hugs and kisses on my cheeks? The love of the people of the north? Maybe all that is love! But I have not found any of it in my life to love. And if I had, it would soon disappear, get lost and nothing would remain, as if it had been a dream, or something imagined, coming toward me from a very long time ago. It is as if I did not live with her, or see her with my own eyes, or hear her with my own ears. It is as if all of this has transpired in a dream or in my mind.

Distances, the greenness, the water and the smell of the sea. I look beyond the fence and I see the cemetery. Scattered graves with their white-washed domes amid the desolation. Families of the dead come from time to time to freshen up the paint. They want the domes to remain white: the whiteness of the tomb is the whiteness of the soul, the whiteness of memory as death obliterates envy and pain, the whiteness of the heart, the whiteness of the day and night of the dead, whiteness of the thoughts of their families: all this is the whiteness of the tombs. All the graves that I have seen or dreamt of had no resemblance to one another. This is a white cemetery. Trees of cactus and lote. The dead do not smell. No fear, no apprehension, no secrets to this graveyard.

When I saw a Christian cemetery I thought it was a garden. I was small then, and I would leave elementary school and accompany the shepherds. Our steps would lead us to the Christian cemetery. All this happened in the south. We could smell the essence of oranges and lemons from the fields and climb over the metal fence so we could walk amongst the flowers and along the clean paved pathways. The guard would hand us cakes and smile as he drank wine from a flask. He would not allow the goats to enter, but he would let us in. White marble, the inscriptions, the pathways, the crosses, the flowers. Everything will dissipate, as if the dead were taking walks in these gardens.

There were no Jews in our small town in the south. When I found out that the doctor was a Spanish Jew I did not care. He would smile as he attended to the sick. He would ask about illness with downcast eyes. He was afraid of the eyes of the nurses and the sick. He spoke little, but the medicine he handed out was good. He allowed me to visit the Jewish cemetery after we had gone for a walk on the stony beach. He said that the tombstones were poems, elegies, written by the dead for the dead at moments when the fingers of time slipped from one tombstone or another. I did not understand anything he said. He talked to himself as he approached some tombs, running his fingers over the writing. He would say: "Here are the tears of separation, the songs, the stories, the pulse, the nights, the desires, and the water drops of life. Over here are the candles, the fluttering eyelashes, the kisses and whispers, what one neighbour told another." He would stop at some of the marble tombstones and I would walk ahead a little; I did not care what he murmured to himself. I asked him if he had any dead relatives in the cemetery, but he did not answer except to murmur repeatedly, "Pulse, tears, fluttering eyelashes, candles," so I left him talking to himself, telling himself what he wanted, and allowed a distance between us as we walked through the cemetery.

Did the doctor die? Did I kill him? He was afraid of getting killed though he never expressed this fear to anyone. He never spoke of his private affairs. Is it possible that I could have been one of those who had killed the doctor? I had not loved him in that lethal way of the people of the north; but then who knows, maybe I killed him! I don't know. Maybe he died or got killed, I don't know.

Here are the bags of vegetables and fruits. I did not buy meat. I will fry some fish that I have in the fridge. I don't like the meat of the north. It has no taste. I remember the lamb of the south, mother's cooking, the fried food. We would eat meat one or two days a week, but we would smell its cooked aroma every day in the streets and alleyways. The south of the crossing. All trucks and cargo travel south, drivers and passengers love the meat of the south. I never smelled the aroma of that southern cooking in the north. In the north I smelled burning human flesh. It was on a summer afternoon, fire consumed the flesh and then charred the bones after the clothes, the hair and the flesh had burned. He was twitching, rolling on the ground and screaming in despair until the burnt body stilled in one place and the flame continued smouldering. No one came near. I alone screamed and bit my fingers, unable to get close. That was all in a dream, after a burnt man came to the hospital and after I saw his deformed body. He died a few hours later. I dreamt that night of the smell, which I continued to recognise in the house and everywhere for several days. I slept and woke to dreams with confused images, events, gestures, furtive movements, and of places I never saw in my life.

One time I woke up and I remembered the dream of the wall where a layer of paint had been burned off and fire had penetrated the brick. I sensed the wall moving, moaning, twitching, as if it wanted to leave its place and move closer to the water. The wall started to have human features: hopping, complaining and trying to move away from the fire. No fire. The fire remained in his body as he continued burning. I smelled the burning of a man as the wall acquired two terrified eyes popping out of their holes with the fire coming close to them. But it was a wall: precisely that of the café, and I recognised the plates, the cups, the glasses, the cafeteria and that was in the north. I just knew it was the north without anything indicating that. Then the wall started to cry. Tears

67

streaming as he continued looking at me. The smell of burning, the crackling, the layers of burnt paint falling on the ground with smouldering smoke. The eyes are burnt out, fire consuming, dark smoke coming out of the mouth and nostrils filling the café with its density and from his waist the smell of burning flesh.

*This is the cemetery*
*tombstones, domes, eyes of owls.*
*lote trees and cactus.*

I remember the cemetery of the south where the "mule of the grave" emerges on its three hooves screaming and wild, terrifying the dead; disturbing their nights; pushing them toward madness; dissipating their gatherings and silencing their stories and their secrets. When they see her moving stealthily between the tombstones, they start begging, supplicating, knowing that now the hour of punishment has come. The three hooves, the terrified screams, the untamed beast. No one can banish her from the cemetery. Laughter dies, stories die, curses and gossip die, everything dies and only supplication remains. Is that why she arrived? This is the cemetery of the south. Here in the north they have cemeteries for cats and dogs. In the south, the domes of the cemetery are perforated with four holes and empty of a mausoleum. They are simply domes spread out through the cemetery, I don't know why. Maybe to fill up a hardened space for the eyes or to create a wider expanse for the imagination. Is it the imagination of the dead, or the imagination of the living? Or the imagination of the doctor?

Scattered domes; not one faces the other. We can forget their existence as long as it means nothing. Maybe the souls enter and leave it in an unending journey beginning with open doors and ending at the same doors. Coming and going. Leaving from the entrance and coming in from the exit looking for the lost body or for the self. They never named these domes after a saint, a mediator, a wali. The wali lost his grave and entered oblivion. How many nights have I had nightmares about the cemetery of the south which I saw as a child? I learnt later that it was a graveyard for the murdered, the insane, for prostitutes and killers, for the homeless, and I did not want to be buried there. At one time that cemetery did not terrify my nights, I used to walk through it often without hearing or seeing anything.

The bags of vegetables and fruits are weighing heavily on my hands. I heave one breath, my heart beat increases. I touch my forehead; it is wet with cold sweat. I gasp and the vegetables and fruit fall from my hands. I probably remained standing there.

*Translated by Mona Zaki*

# The Companion

## MOHAMMED DIB

God bless you, good people all! No lack of good humour here! Are we not in the prime of life, sturdy, of sound mind? What more do you need? The earth is long and wide; there's a place for everyone in it; everyone can live here as he pleases, any way he likes. Great is our mother Algeria, may blessings rain upon her! And many of our kind are very sympathetic to us: this we shall proclaim before the entire universe, as long as a breath of life remains in us. Our brothers have never allowed to die of starvation the creature you see before you. Yes! the whole world knows us. We are like the bird that sips water from the fountain and nests in the tiles. Some, the majority call us Djeha, and others, friends and acquaintances, Djahdjouh.

Oh, the things they've said about us! They all know some tale concerning us; simple minds and intellectuals alike rejoice in our vicissitudes; strolling players, never short of imagination, invent fresh stories about the trials we suffer. And all because, may God forgive me, never once was I able to hold my tongue.

To tell the truth, I spread the good word among those who have no wish to hear it: merchants, fat bellies, the holier-than-thou, pious frauds, the great ones who know heaven is not as high as they are, fake savants, the lowly ones when they have the souls of slaves. The poor, I swear, have never been attacked by me! The poor are already sufficiently trodden underfoot. I hope that will weigh in the favour of a sinner like me. And what if I have blustered and bragged beyond all reason, pooh! that's simply because at bottom I'm just a hopeless nincompoop. But all that's a lot of wind. What I really want is to tell you the tale of misadventure, the most recent to befall your poor old Djeha . . .

Well, that individual, I can still see him in my mind's eye, was dressed in a manner not suited to our land – he was wearing more clothes than necessary, and all very dark in tone – came up to me one afternoon when I was taking my customary stroll through the town, and asked:

"Djeha?"

"In person," I admitted, as I was endeavouring to think of what sort of countenance to adopt faced with this stranger.

"I know you!"he said.

"Who doesn't know Djeha, young man!"

"But I know you in a special way."

Whereupon he gave me a wink.

"Well, really . . ."

"You came to our district once . . . I was still a kid, really."

"Where haven't I been, son . . . If these feet could speak!"

All the same, I began to feel a bit worried. I looked the man in the face: "Whatever will he bring out next?" I was thinking: he had such shining eyes, they were like blazing coals.Though he was short and slender, this man, still young, seemed possessed of a great nervous strength.While talking to me, his fine-featured face crinkled in amusement and a wave of wrinkles played on his hard, narrow forehead.

My inspection did not seem to disturb him. He went on:

"You had described your adventures to a group of locals who were considerably entertained by them. One of them, Uncle Salim, wanting to show his appreciation, had brought you a magnificent live cock . . ."

All the time he was speaking, he kept blinking his eyes; I kept my distance. In spite of some incomprehensible surge of sympathy that brought me closer to him, I refused to let him blarney me. This youngster was doubtless some shameless farceur. But whether it was the frank smile that made his eyes sparkle from within, or else the suddenly aroused desire to know how far this fortuitous encounter would lead me, I was won over. Was there not some more serious reason for it? I no longer recall what it was that persuaded me to lend him a sympathetic ear.

I answered with as much detachment as I could muster:

"It may well have been so, but anyhow I no longer remember."

"They had all drifted away," my interlocutor continued, paying no heed to what I'd said. "There I was alone beside you. I kept gazing at you in wonder, telling myself: 'It's Djeha!' I might have stood forever staring at you wide-eyed if you had not suddenly looked at me, beckoned to me to approach you, then whispered in my ear: 'Here, lad, take this cock. Take it to your mother; get her to make you a good couscous with it.' You put the bird into my hands and strode away hurriedly."

Now I looked at this companion with even greater curiosity and we started to chat.

He soon told me all about himself, telling me he'd just arrived, that very day, from across the sea. From France! After a four-year absence, he had taken a holiday, and had returned to see the old country. And his family, too: his wife and three children. These, he explained, were all boys; in his eyes, the pride he felt at this made a joyous flame start dancing. But it had not been easy to return home. He was afraid of not being able to recognise them: "Four years, dear soul, just think! I could feel something terrible stirring within me. I was terrified at the idea that soon I would be confronting them."

All at once, my doubts disappeared. How well I understood his heart! All the same, he could not bring himself to talk to me about his wife, even though it was obvious he never stopped thinking of her. It is not the custom, in our land, for a man to speak of his wife. What a stupid idea! What? Is it a

72

shameful defect, to have a beautiful and loving wife? That's husbands for you – idiots!

If you want to talk in comfort, there's nothing better than sitting down to a good brew of fresh tea, is there? So I suggested to the young man that we should go and relax in a café. But he seemed very upset, for he refused outright to go one step of the way with me. He said that it was he who should invite me, and would be very honoured if I would accept: he was really sorry that he hadn't thought about it first.

"All right, if that's all it takes to please you," I replied.

And he calmed down. Naturally, he had not understood that my proposition was just out of politeness. I didn't have a penny to my name. Yet his whole attitude had aroused in me such a strong feeling of friendship that, without realising what I was letting myself in for, I hadn't been able to resist inviting him. In any case, he would have paid for the drinks, out of consideration for me, I'm sure.

In fact, there was something else. Have you ever noticed that at certain moments we long to demonstrate our gratitude to someone because of a rush of happiness that makes the heart as light as a bubble? So it was with this young man.

Seated in the courtyard of an old funduq, we were drinking some excellent tea. It was the end of November, still mild. From the four corners of the building entirely occupied by craftsmen were coming the songs and dhikr or religious chants of slipper-makers, the swallow-cries of the weavers' shuttles, the nasal whine of leather merchants coming and going. Birds were chirping in their cages; others, flying free, were answering them from the top of a pomegranate tree growing there. All at once, I relaxed and gave myself up to the sense of peace that came from this buzzing of a busy hive all around us.

Suddenly my companion, who had remained in silence until then, asked me: "Is everything really all right with you here?"

This question suddenly shot at me, made me jump. I had not been expecting such a question on the part of my comrade. It made a sharp contrast with the agreeable sensation of well-being that the surroundings had instilled in my soul! Shaking his curly head, the young man, who had already told me his name was Zubir, leaned towards me. I gave him a penetrating look: his lively expression seemed to me quite honest. But it was difficult for me to guess what he was getting at.

Nevertheless, I inwardly felt that all was not well with us. In fact, things were worsening.

Without waiting for my answer, he declared: "Here's what things are like now in this place: you have laws, plenty of laws, but no justice, no truth . . ."

There now gleamed in his eyes looks as piercing as daggers. He spoke with simplicity and conviction. Impossible not to believe this man. I listened to him. The things he talked about created within me a dull alarm, an unease growing hard to bear.

After a brief pause, he added, his face darkening: "I know it's bad to become an expatriate. I deserted my country, but do you think I did so with a light heart? There was nothing else I could do. I'm strong, clever with my hands, but I couldn't find anything here in the way of work."

He started to laugh. Praise heaven! How delighted I felt to see him in a less sombre mood; his eyes, so serious, now flashed with pure goodness of heart.

But at once he began again: "I was never able to find suitable work. Odd jobs, yes, but never real work that gives you satisfaction when you've finished it, never! So I left! Since then, my children have begun to eat their fill. They do not see their father, but at least they have something to eat. I've saved a little money, too."

As he said that, he laughed openly.

"Peanuts!" he grumbled. "And yet . . . it's something after all."

At first I could not understand why his laugh sounded so extraordinary. He was young, of course. At that age, all you need is a sudden touch of humour for everything good in you to express itself in your face. So a man who is able to work, to buy food for his family and still save a little — such a man is something wonderful.

Such were the feelings that gradually arose within me. I was smiling at my companion; he was smiling also whenever his eyes met mine.

In the end, I had to tell him:"That's admirable. True, you're still rather young; but you have character and you'll be a success."

"I'm not so sure," he replied simply.

"Above all, love your fellow man, but look him full in the face. In that way, even if he has wicked intentions, he'll leave you alone."

"I get on well with all men, except my father-in-law, who has the tongue of a viper, and all people in authority."

Surprised, I took another good look at my companion. And I thought: "Ah, what it is to be young! The young have their pride, they know what they want! Look at yourself, Djeha, the way you muddle everything up and never know which way to turn."

I could feel his presence warming my old heart. It was such unexpected happiness, undeserved, to have such a being sitting beside me. In my young days, we did not talk like that; young people know only a narrow, tedious existence, a useless existence!

I seem to see him again as he appeared before my eyes. His image will never be wiped out of my memory; I can see the green cape he was wearing: it did not reach right down to his knees, but was tied at the waist by a wide belt. His boyish face with the sharp features was crowned by a voluminous head of black, curly hair on which he wore neither cap nor chechia. His shining eyes spread a comforting light all round him.

Alas, sadness and joy live side by side, and under the same

roof. After a few minutes of silence, during which Zubir seemed to be recalling his entire past life, he scratched his head, sighed, and continued, his eyes looking into the distance: "All the same, there is so much misery in this country, it's difficult to know where to start talking about it. You realise that especially when, like me, you've just come back from a land where everyone works, makes money and enjoys life."

Once again, I felt uneasy. The self-assurance of his criticisms, the maturity of the reflections he expressed, obviously produced a surprising effect. But as he delivered those words, an expression of unbearable tension appeared on his face. When I saw that, I felt an absurd anxiety. He went on talking, and began to tell me about his father. He had been a coffee-grinder. Zubir wanted to show me – he upon whom fate had smiled – just what had been the sort of life his own father had led.

"Today," he said, "you can go anywhere and find your coffee ground in a few seconds by a machine. In my childhood, things were different. A man had to use all his strength to reduce to the finest powder – finer than flour – the coffee beans. And my father had that task!"

As he was speaking, his fist clenched violently as if seizing some invisible enemy. I for my part remained silent. I did not want to interrupt him while he was struggling to collect his memories.

"My father had to work in a deep, dark hole, a sort of ditch at the end of a filthy dead-end impasse. The place was always shut off by a heavy door. Like a prison gate I felt – I don't know why. You could hardly see a thing; it was like being buried alive in the place! The pestle was of solid black iron, I remember it was bigger than me and weighed at least forty pounds. All day long, my father had to lift and drop it without stop, never a pause to rest, until his bones were cracking. He pounded and pounded, with frightful gasping breaths. In the end, he no longer really knew what he was doing. His face would drip with drenching sweat, and its black rivulets would gleam faintly on his forehead, his cheeks, his withered neck. He was already old; his sight was dimming and he was becoming blind. The hollows of his eyes also filled with blackish sweat. You could have sworn that they were tears dripping from his wrinkled eyelids, and that those tears were black. There was great sadness in him, but he went on pounding, pounding, and panting heavily. Every blow he delivered in the enormous mortar reverberated right through his chest."

I could no longer bear what he was telling me, I felt annihilated by his tale, and yet I was all ears. If I had not felt ashamed to do so, I would have howled with pity there among all the craftsmen's workshops, amid all the comings and goings around us.

That boy was tearing at my very heart. "This is our life," I told myself, "and that is the life our brothers have to endure!" And the repressed sobs caught in my throat were strangling me like a hangman's rope.

But the young man kept on:

"Sometimes, unable to go on, my father would collapse, with his nose against the ground. He was glad to be in that position, I'm sure. But I was put there to supervise him. I had to stay with him all day long. So I would set him on his feet again at once, for fear that the boss might come along and find him flat on the ground. And I would tell myself: 'You've used up all your strength, my poor father. You'll have to take a rest, or die.' But above all I could not allow myself to feel such compassion for him. I could not allow him to rest his aching limbs on the earth that would one day receive them. If I had, he himself would later have scolded and punished me. So I would wipe his face with a rag and, using all my strength, lift him up and put the pestle back in his groping hands. As he started work again, he would whisper: 'Thanks, son.'

"His energy would return and then one could hear the regular pounding of the pestle in a tranquil rhythm, a slightly dull sound, that shook the foundations of the old houses all round us. He would even start a discussion with me; in fact, he was not by nature a sad person. Though he would express himself in the bitterest terms, it was not sadness that made him do it . . ."

Having reached this point in his tale, my friend stopped speaking for a while and his face took on a hard look.

I gently encouraged him to go on: "Come on, tell the whole story!"

With my encouragement, he began slowly, very slowly, to gather his thoughts again, his gaze under the arched eyebrows fixed straight ahead of him. He seemed so pitiable! As I listened to him mumbling like that, I became overwhelmed by a strange presentiment, while at the same time there awakened in me an irresistible desire, something never known before, to meditate upon all those things I had heard. Of course it was not the right moment to embark upon such questions. So I decided to await a more propitious moment. His youthful voice, level and slightly subdued, went on:

"Whenever the boss came, several times a day, to collect the powdered coffee, he would shout, as if it was a good joke: 'Ahmed, you're too old; we'll have to find someone younger!'

At first, my father would protest, saying he'd never felt stronger in his life: he seemed to have resigned himself to the fate that awaited him. So after each visit from the boss, invariably I would hear him mutter: 'When I'm blind, I'll go begging and I'll be more happy.' Whenever I heard those words, I would sincerely wish he would lose his sight as soon as possible. I could already see myself guiding him. We would wander over many lands. This project filled me with hope. One day I talked to him about it: he smiled, and answered me: 'That's fine: we'll set off together holding out our hands in the name of God.' But it didn't happen as we had hoped: my father passed away with his hands still gripping the pestle."

The young man fell silent, as if something invisible had suddenly frightened him: his features shuddered and his whole face contracted. He lowered his forehead, and sat without moving. He seemed to be listening to something. After a while, he raised his head. Just when I was least expecting it, he abruptly ended his story with these words:

"It was towards the day's end that it became so terrifying. He would utter such cries of pain and suffering, it was unbearable. It was getting dark then. I would run and call my mother and she and I, each supporting him on one arm, would drag him back home."

I, too, remember a mean, miserable childhood. We were bored, for a soul-extinguishing lassitude emanated from it like an asphyxiating fog. We were so bored, we felt as if we were being stifled: a leaden weight seemed to load down the chest. When I evoke that past, still recent, I find it difficult to believe that it was really like that. Certainly, man was shrouded in a cloak of ignorance and fear. He walked with lowered head; full of timidity, he dared not show himself to the world. And today? Today you can see how he has learnt self-respect, refusing to be humiliated. We have lifted the mourning veil knotted round our hearts. God has given us longer life, all of us, and we shall see better days. Take Djeha's word for it. And when that time comes, it will only be certain individuals who do not have a clear conscience.

To return to my companion, here he is now, happy to be the father of three boys, and to be employed . . .

There we were, talking away, the two of us. It was as if he were re-living a long nightmare during those few moments; he closed his eyes and, as if seized by remorse, wondered: "Why on earth did I let myself be carried away by such memories?"

He had a stricken look. Then he opened his eyes: his face was illuminated by a healing smile.

It was just at that second that I saw the black groups of police rushing into the funduq and descending upon us like a flock of crows. My friends, what can I say? Was this some calamity falling upon us? I did not realise what was happening. Ah, my brethren, what horror! They fell upon us with fists and truncheons hip and thigh. Blows rained down upon us. Those assassins attacked, their metal helmets pulled down to their ears. We received punches to the stomach, blows to legs and backbones. Many people were trying to run away with bloody mouths, others with split heads. Turbans flew off the heads of honorable citizens; peaceful craftsmen were driven out, trampled underfoot; others – me, my companion, in a trice, all of us were arrested and put in chains, as if we were criminals. And for what reason, Almighty God? But it was not until much later, when I emerged from prison, that I understood the reason.

Zubir recovered straight away. After what had happened, manhandled by all those police pigs, it was hard to gather one's wits together, to speak out loud. As for me, I was stunned. But that brave young man called to me quite without emotion: "Are you there? Ah, there you are! Don't be afraid, it's all over . . ."

All over? I held my tongue: I was not as sure as he was. My heart was pounding hard: it was sending me fearsome warnings in an unaccustomed fanfare, distant but clearly perceptible. Anyhow, despite my disarray, I had reason to feel glad, for I had found my companion again. You cannot imagine what a comfort it is in such circumstances to see a friend's face. Little by little, I regained my self-confidence. But by God, sirs, what a rough-and-tumble it was! I don't know whether it was with fright or surprise, but my back was all wet. It could well have been terror, after all.

But it was because we were going to be marched through town under the eyes of the whole population. Oh, the shame . . . I bent my back, kept silent and started walking. Seeing me thus cast down, Zubir questioned me in a low voice as the other captives followed or walked in front of us: "Are you feeling frightened?"

"No."

"It's nothing, really."

At that moment, I had a strange thought. "The café owner," I asked myself, "he served us tea without expecting anything like this would happen. Who's going to pay him, pay for his broken glasses, his shattered chairs, tables, benches?" I imagined him lamenting the useless remains of his business and, may I be forgiven, I could hardly suppress the laughter that started to shake me. Why? It would be difficult to explain. As they say "I laughed till I cried".

That was when I noticed, walking in front of us at the head of the group, the man himself, without his turban that he must have lost in the free-for-all! I recognised at once his rough-hewn Kaimuk head, close-shaven, massive, descending to his neck in thick rolls of flesh covered with prickly hairs. The café owner was marching along as dignified as if accompanying a wedding procession, with lifted chin, that seemed to defy the police by indicating the road they should follow. "Djeha, my boy!" I said to myself, "You simply must adopt the same impressive bearing." So I puffed out my chest, drew my eyebrows down in a frown and went on my way proudly, just like my fellow notable, swinging my arms. At once I felt as if I had grown taller, to be taller than my real height. And I thought to myself: "We are going to see their prison. So what? . . . Men are born to know prison also."

Quite cheered up, I was walking along sustained by these thoughts when, out of the crowd lining our route and gazing at us in respect, a European broke through and rushed upon us. He was foaming at the mouth, the man was yelling at us. Raising his fist above his head, he screamed: "Stop . . . stop! . . ."

Then the beast began to hit out and shriek at us as if he was out of his mind. And we couldn't understand why it was my young friend who received most of the blows. He stepped aside to avoid them; he was trying to defend himself, but his wrists were in handcuffs. And I started shouting: "Arrest that man! For goodness' sake, arrest him!"

No one made a move to do so among the police. From among the curious bystanders a murmur arose. Were we going to be delivered from this raving madman, yes or no? The police raised their pistols, pointed on one side at us, on the other at the crowd. The crowd fell silent; it made no further movement. At that very moment I finally felt fear, and an irrational panic seized me. The European, protected by the police pistols, went on punching our comrade. I was observing everything, including myself, as if detached from my body, in an unbelievable state of divided personality; nevertheless, I cannot confirm that I remained self-possessed. Suddenly Zubir uttered a groan: a faint, horrible sound, the dull sound made by a branch snapping. He waved his chained hands in the air, reared up and then fell to the grounds dragging me down with him in his collapse. He was shaking all over, but uttered no sound. Arching his back higher, he stretched his neck and looked towards me: his eye shot a demented gleam whose horror no human tongue could describe. Then his head fell back. I was stretched almost full-length beside him.

The man went on raining blows upon him. He was yelling: "Think I'm going to let you off alive, you bastard!"

My brethren, I had never guessed that a human heart could contain so much hatred. That day, I saw things your eyes would never believe. Heaven save us from such madness, silence that voice within us.

I should be telling lies if I described to you how we were able to go on our way: from that moment on, the succession of events grows dim, becomes vague in my mind. All the same, a few isolated facts remain engraved in my memory with a maddening precision, while others drift around in a capriciously moving mist. For example, I only imperfectly recall how we got on our feet and what state we were in as we prisoners, supporting our companion, struggled on our way as best we could . . .

It was a way that led us to the prison. Pain had gripped my

shoulders like a savage beast of prey. I dragged myself along, stunned; I was appalled by the noise my companion's bones had made as they broke in his crumpled suit all covered with dirt so it resembled an old sack. And within myself, the fine flame of fraternity I had felt for all the world was extinguished; I was wandering in bottomless obscurity. Zubir's head was banging against my chest, his back was bent double, his arms dangled; he was no longer walking, we were simply carrying him.

After that, I do not know what happened.

When I came to myself, I was hurting all over. My body was drenched as if several buckets of water had been thrown over me, but a water that was filthy and with a sickening stench. My head was swollen, hanging down heavily: it was still throbbing with that great uproar. I only wanted to say nothing, see nothing: everything seemed to me so horrible. A great number of strangers were piled in beside us in a long, narrow cell: all lay stretched out, motionless, like freshly-sawn tree trunks; a few still had the strength to groan with pain. I waited: I could hear the sound of water running not far away. As I lay there, I gazed on my surroundings, understanding nothing, my thoughts wandering. After a few minutes, I could make out a few faces, hairy, grey, stuck to the cement floor. Somewhere, in a far corner, or through a wall – but where in fact – someone was watching. Yet I could see no one there. It was like a face lost in the half-darkness and turning its rolling eyes upon me; I had a great desire to sit up, despite the curious feebleness that drained my limbs, in order to study the face better. But, rooted to the spot, I was unable to move, not even to lift an arm. Suddenly a need to escape took an irrepressible hold upon me. Then I managed to realise the monstrousness of the situation I was in: daylight dawned in my mind, and I thought to myself: "Djeha, Djeha, what's happening, to you. Where have you got yourself now? Poor old Djeha! . . ."

I could not resist the impulse that at once urged me to raise myself from the ground. Then barely had I managed to sit up, a prolonged howling made me jump out of my torpor. I cast frantic looks about me. It was not coming from our cell: it was strange! Anyhow, it gave me such a shock, I fell back full-length again on the ground, powerless, almost losing consciousness. In my semi-consciousness, I realised that there were prisoners on the other side of the wall. At the same moment a door banged shut, making the dark, massive building shudder, footsteps slithered along a corridor and a long death-rattle lingered in the silence. I curled up in my corner. Those noises began again, a wave of sound again penetrating the whole building. After that a mournful, rhythmical complaint, rising above the nearer death-rattle, let itself be heard for a long time before dying away in total exhaustion. Lying on my belly, I listened, panting, staring at something in front of me, and what I saw made me almost lose my mind.

There on the floor Zubir was lying, face upwards; his clenched fists, the thumbs inside, were laid on his chest. His eyes, which had lost their brilliance, looked like congealed fat. Yet his eyebrows were arched very high, as if he were still telling the tragic story of his father to some invisible listener. That look was growing very strange; it seemed extinct yet it was still obstinately riveted to the ceiling's murky pallor. Then I could see the gaping mouth; its blackened lips were letting brownish rivulets of blood trail from their corners and all along the cheeks and the neck. The blood had formed a sombre puddle under the young man's head. Zubir was motionless. The blood kept trickling out of him without cease: it was almost as if my companion was melting away. Suddenly it felt very cold in the place, and I was seized by a peculiar sense of horror. Jaws clamped tight, I grew numb.

Later – much later, it seemed to me – I saw that they had moved me to another place: the setting in which I now found myself was quite different. I was in a spacious hall, well-lit, along with other people of course. My companion had disappeared; there were no more traces of blood on the floor.

What had become of him? I questioned those near me, but none of them could answer my question; some did not even know what I was talking about. And it is quite likely that they took me for someone whose mind had become unhinged by all those events. I could see from the expressions on their faces that they seemed to feel sorry for me. It was all just beginning!

But then I learned that we were going to be put through an interrogation: we had been tidied up and brought there for that purpose. At once, a powerful voice began calling people's names: they were the first to have to appear before the authorities.

When my turn finally arrived and I presented myself, a man seated behind a big desk began to shake his head and grumble something: then he shouted: "Dja-kha! Dja-kah! What sort of a name is that? What's this nincompoop doing here? Yet another crazy bastard! Go on, get out of here!"

When he uttered these last words, which his foul breath spat in my face, he raised his eyes. What a head, what a look! . . . He was just another creature like ourselves, you might say. Yet if all the world were like that, we would have reason to fear man, and to fear for mankind.

I was pondering these thoughts and they were far from joyful until I forgot even the presence of this representative of law and order, so incongruous did it all seem to me. Suddenly, I was seized by the collar, shoved without ceremony to the exit, and there I received a boot up the backside. The cop who chucked me out must have had long experience of that sort of treatment of his fellow men.

As if by magic, I found myself back once more in the street, surrounded by the comings and goings of passers-by going about their affairs — itinerant salesmen who rent the air with their endless cries from street to street, kids scuffling like frenzied sparrows, cars rushing at top speed without any consideration for pedestrians. The crowd's powerful current engulfed me, carried me along with it among countless cries, countless noises, hysterical bicycle bells, voluptuous popular songs spewing out from café gramophones, donkey-men yelling at the tops of their voices "Balak! Balak!"and the battering of open-air cobblers' hammers. Finding myself mingling with human beings, hearing all that free and easy way of living, filling my lungs with fresh air without paying a penny for it, feeling on my back God's good sun, shining warm even though it was almost winter – well now, should I confess it? – I felt neither happy nor satisfied.

Was I not free? Was I not like those pigeons I saw hopping here and there on the street, peck-pecking here and there, then, suddenly scared away, rising up into the air in which they flew around so gracefully one never wearied of admiring them? Was not I, too, going to return to my old way of life, and, like those birds, "drink at the fountain and nest in the tiles?" I didn't know. I no longer really knew.

Certainly, I was not at all disposed to take up my former habits, and the thought never even entered my mind. No, I still did not feel I was a free man! I am incapable of explaining what was happening to me, but that was the sort of thing I was feeling. I still had the impression of being back in my dark cell, crammed to suffocation with my companions in misfortune. On the streets, it could be said that I was transporting my prison with me, on my back, or that my soul had also been cast into prison and had stayed there, while I was making my way through the great world unfettered. I walked all over the town; and disconnected ideas, catastrophic ideas, crowded and bustled around my aching brain.The good people who saw me passing by, and they all, praise be to God, so many of them who still remembered their good friend Djeha and waved him greetings, found themselves ignored, and nodded their heads sadly. One of them complained loud enough for me to hear him say, "That's what prison does to you!"Ah! how well he understood my condition!

I went on wandering a long time in that state: how many hours? Who could say? The thick, suffocating heat of

November without a cloud was weighing the city down. The image of my dead companion kept reappearing in front of me, his blood started running again before my eyes. Something went on swelling up in my head and in my heart . . . All that had happened because, as I had realised a few minutes before being booted out of the prison, all that was because protesters had risen up to defend their land. Then a strange calm descended upon me, my head became quite cold. A lucidity, a feeling of unbelievable strength, a sort of wild enthusiasm like some terrible chant invaded my soul. Our brethren over there in the mountains – have they given up their arms against the vermin that devoured the interior of our eyeballs? What do you believe will happen next? Every day will see fresh combatants going to join them!

*Translated from the French*
*by James Kirkup*

# Provisions of Sand

## SAID AL-KAFRAWI

I passed the clock in the Midan that indicated it was long past midnight. The metallic chime reminded me that it has been a long time and that returning home to my ancestors meant that I had arrived at the end of the line.

I crossed Hanafi Street. An old blind man was sitting in the Midan on a wooden bench reciting Sufi prayers by himself. I walked up to the open kiosk that was lit with neon lights. It had jars of sweets, small boxes, each piece in a silver wrapping, a Qur'anic verse – its gilded letters reflecting the dim light through a narrow wooden frame; the owner inside resisting sleep.

"A packet of cigarettes".

He threw it to me. I lit one. "Has the stop for Kafr al-Higazi changed?"

"Oh, a long time ago".

Silence. I looked at his bulging eyes, his wide mouth, his dark features, his head wrapped in a scarf. He was fighting the fatigue of a long night with an exhausted yawn. "The last bus leaves at midnight. Take a taxi."

I turned my back standing for a moment on the pavement. A gust of cold wind stirred the dust up. I looked at the fading advert for the "Spiritual Brotherhood", one I had often read as a child. A longing hit my heart. I realised that after many years I was returning a different man from the one who left.

The kiosk man shouted after me: "It's late and it looks like you're a stranger round here. The road to the Kafr at night is dangerous. Spend the night at a hotel and the morning is another day."

I smiled and he heard me say "God is the helper". I took one step and added: "I have to go home."

He lay his head down and slept. I walked the empty street and thought how many times I had crossed it in the past searching for a refuge. I raised my hand: "Taxi!"

The cab stopped and a small head peered out of the window. "Yes?"

"I want to go to Kafr Higazi."

"Yes?"

"Kafr Higazi".

"Now?"

"Did I say tomorrow?"

"Did anyone tell you that my life is worthless!"

His answer surprised me. Accelerating away, he screamed in my face. "Kafr Higazi! And in the middle of the night!!"

The screeching tyres of his wheels made a noise like a wail. I walked down a street shaded on both sides by trees. A cold autumn with lights reflecting on the uneven asphalt of the road. The advertisement for Cinema Misr on its metal legs was terrifying and alive as if painted by ghosts from the lake.

Leaving the town behind, I walked to the path by the river from where one took the ferry-boat, the only way of getting from here to the village. The moment my foot sank in the sand, I whispered to myself: "That's it! The trap."

Unconsciously, I found myself walking in a far from indifferent night – overpowered by the darkness I had feared as a child. As I sat on top of the old oven, my grandmother would tell me stories about djinn and the inhabitants of the underworld.

One night that carefree child went to his mother as she sat kneading and spreading out the dough, hitting the surface monotonously like a drum. He approached with an outstretched hand asking for his pocket money. She looked up and said: "For the movies, of course. Oh, you scamp!"

She raised her right arm and he put his hand in her pocket, grabbed the coin and ran. Before he reached the door he heard her say: "Watch out for the Sidra and the night."

"Again, mother?"

"I told you a thousand times the Queen of the Djinn lives in the gorge. She comes out at night and sits on the hill under the Sidra combing her hair in the moonlight and singing 'A bride waiting for a bridegroom!' She waits for those returning, bewitches them and drags them to the bottom of the deep."

It scared me and I hesitated, but my passion for the coloured pictures sent me to my room to quickly change my work clothes and put my shoes on. At the movies, I got carried away and only came back to earth when the lights were turned on. I dashed to the door to find the lights of the town dimmed, shadows reflecting on the walls. Then I remembered the Sidra and the Queen of the Djinn and was scared to go to the place where the ferry-boat was moored.

The ferry-boat was operated by iron chains and a metal pulley. It was owned by Captain Abd al-Qadir whom I loved like a father. I called out to him from the edge of town: "Captain Abd al-Qadir! I want to go home!" His tall thin frame emerged pulling on the chains. I heard the metallic clang and his singing. His deep voice echoed across the water; then he shouted out: "So it's you! Let's see how things will end up with you!" His voice coming across the night disoriented me, and in fear I imagined that Captain Abd al-Qadir was transformed into several people singing. His shadow moved with the wind which was stirring the glow of his fire. I jumped onto the ferry-boat and he handed me a glass of tea, and poked the small fire I had seen in the distance. Water and fire were his companions.

He gazed at me — a huddled heap next to the rudder; he sucked his lips and said:

"You boy, you spit of an afreet! Don't you ever see sense?

90

What will you come to, every week a different story!"

"It's the last time, Captain Abd al-Qadir!"

"Listen here, you good-for-nothing! I know that your head is like a bee-hive and that you are not like the other children in the village. Your head's full of things I do not know. You will come to regret this. Staying up till the midnight hour is dangerous for a child your age."

"Do you mean the Sidra and the djinn?"

"Of course."

"The one who sings 'A bride for a bridegroom', bewitching people with her drums and music and taking them to the far, far deep?"

"Of course, the amazing thing is that you know everything."

"But I never saw her, Captain Abd al-Qadir."

"You are lucky. But you will and it will make you sterile. Last month she grabbed Mustafa Abu Nadi and nailed him to the Sidra, and sat watching the river and combing her hair. When Mustafa saw her enormous breasts he lunged at them, sucking her milk and begging for forgiveness. At that very moment she told him: 'Now you have tasted my milk your life is valueless to me' and she let him go. Had he not done that he would have been taken, just like that!"

The story of Mustafa so terrified me that I steered the rudder in the wrong direction. Looking at me, Captain Abd al-Qadir added: "And you – if the one God permits – will have the same fate. The djinniya will nail your penis to the Sidra and slice your balls off as they do to the rams."

He laughed at my fear. The moon came out from behind the clouds and I spotted the other bank. I jumped off and started running, screaming out: "Thanks a lot, Captain Abd al-Qadir! Just this time! No one got hurt! Say hello to the Queen of the Djinn for me!" His laughter followed me, and so did his curses.

After all these years, his laughter rings in my soul. I was

amazed that coming back these memories were still alive in me. I turned left and saw the sand dunes, the brick moulds, and the river bank. I walked up to the mooring and remembered the mulberry trees and the Sidra on the hill by the river. I rested my foot on a rock and watched the river flowing down to the great sea. I lit another cigarette, waiting to cross to my birthplace. I said to myself: "How many times have you crossed that river? Now you look around in disbelief as if you're a ghost looking at an old memory, filled with desire to put back together what has been torn away. Your guides in the night used to be the light of the fire, the sound of the chains and the ringing laughter of the old man."

The coffee shop's mud walls were cracked and splintered. I called out: "Captain Abd al-Qadir!" The sound echoed, hitting the walls of the night, crossing the years as if it was yesterday.

"Captain Abd al-Qadir!"

It would be a disaster if he had gone home. I sighed and wished that I could grab the first ray of daylight, that I could sit on the bridge at the eastern side of the village by the house where once grandfathers gathered around the brass tray for dinner.

"Captain Abd al-Qadir! I want to go home!"

The sound rang out over the water like a bell; the old fire was out. On the other side nothing moved. A dim light from the coffee shop, some movement and a whisper from within. The door opened a crack and a paraffin lamp reflected on the ground the shadow of a woman.

I gazed at the walls of the coffee-house I had once known; two grimy wooden shelves holding some shabby oddments, a stand with a primus stove, a large metal kettle without a lid, tea glasses stacked in two higgledy-piggledy rows, and on the floor jute sacking and a cushion gleaming with dirt. In a corner, a rumpled cover where someone had slept.

A woman asked: "Who are you calling for, brother?"

I somehow knew the voice, its steady, sleepy tone.

"I am calling for Captain Abd al-Qadir."

The river at my feet continued to ripple in widening circles as fish came to the surface, and from the village a smell I could not identify.

"Abd al-Qadir? Are you a stranger?"

"No, I am from here."

"From here? Whose son are you?"

"I'm from the Badarwa family. I am Ramzi."

"Ramzi? Amina's son? My dear boy, you've been away a long time. Don't you recognise me, Ramzi? I'm Aunt Ifrag, the wife of your Uncle Ibrahim al-Mansi, the coffee-maker."

I suddenly remembered her. Her aged appearance alarmed me. "How are you, Aunt Ifrag? How are you doing?"

She crossed the threshold toward me, her shadow joined mine, sharing the square of light. She had really aged. The unexpected presence of her wrinkled old face was a living example of what had passed. The past was present in a terrifying form.

A shiver went through my body, when I heard her say: "Captain Abd al-Qadir (May God grant you a long life!) . . . He died a long, long time ago."

The light moved and quivered with the wind. A migrating bird screeched as it flew high between sky and earth, and a feeling of loss overwhelmed me.

"He died?"

"Yes. You are calling on the dead, Ramzi, my boy."

"And the ferry-boat, Aunt Ifrag?"

"That went too. Once in a while it comes to transfer workers to the textile factory. It stays on the other side for a day. They have cars now. Come inside and call it a day. Do you remember when you used to sleep here a long time ago?"

"Yes, I do. Thanks, but I'll go back across the bridge."

"That's a long way and it's dark now." She closed her door.

The darkness was all-engulfing. I was alone again. I told myself there is a difference between dreaming and recalling the past. I said to myself: "You're coming back after this

93

absence from what you know. What do you know?"

The old Sidra appeared on the hill stretching its branches over the road, haunting with its shadows and fears. As a child, when I used to reach it I would shiver in fear, fling my arms into the air and avert my eyes so I would not see what I did not want to see. I would clench the hem of my djellaba between my teeth and flee from the terror of the place.

The wind blew suddenly. What a strange thing – to smell the scent of fresh flowers, like perfume! My senses sharpened, I asked myself where that sweet fragrance was coming from? The earth lit up as the moon emerged from behind the clouds. I gazed intently at the Sidra and the hill. My hair stood on end, my body electrified. The Queen of the Djinn that Captain Abd al-Qadir had told me about and whom my mother used to scare me with, and whom I had never seen as a child, took form before me. It was neither my imagination nor an optical illusion. She sat with her huge breasts enveloping her body, combing her long hair – the sound of her singing coming clearly through the night, "A bride waiting for a bridegroom".

For the man who had come from a past destined to perish, stood aghast like one demented, his gaping mouth unable to assimilate the form emerging before him.

*Translated by Mona Zaki*

# *The Visit*

## HABIB SELMI

### 1

"The cities have devoured you," he said, pulling up a chair and sitting on it in the middle of my little room. "You've lost so much weight," he added, lighting his pipe with a pencil-shaped lighter. "Your face is pale and drawn, the brightness of your eyes is gone, but you've become more handsome than ever."

I looked at the lighter he put down on the little table between us. I heard his lips smack as he sipped his coffee, and I heard his cup clink as he returned it to the saucer.

"Your mother says that you've not visited her for a long time and that she misses you; but she doesn't know that you live in a beautiful home in the heart of the city."

At that moment, it occurred to me to get rid of him but I didn't, not out of pity for him, but fearing those painful feelings that take hold of me on doing something wrong.

### 2

There he was, in front of me. The distance between us was no more than a metre. His body was piled on the chair, his shirt open and showing his bulging chest. He talked to me in the same manner as he did ten years ago, as though he had not changed, as though he still was that child I loved in those

95

distant years.

When he phoned, I had immediately invited him to come. I dictated my address to him clearly: the metro station, the street, the district, the number of the building and the floor. I described the entrance to him accurately. I told him that the porter always waxed the stairs, and I advised him to hold on to the railing as he went up, lest he should slip.

And here he was now, in front of me, a heavy body piled on a little chair. And here I was, wondering about the reasons that made me invite him, and trying to persuade myself that there was still something that bound me to him and impelled me to silence that inner voice ordering me to kick him out.

## 3

He bent over the table, stretching his head which appeared to me then like that of a startled tortoise. He picked up the lighter and thrust it in the pocket of his trousers. He took another sip of coffee and I heard the smack of his lips, again. A moment later, he pulled back his upper body and began staring at me.

"Your mother said that your teeth were late to come through and that your uncle used to repeat jokingly that you would remain without teeth."

He took the pipe out of his mouth and laughed. I became aware that his right foot almost touched my left. I thought of stepping on it, and then of what he might do if I actually did.

## 4

Suddenly, the sunshine filled the room. I got up and turned off the light, then returned to my chair. He let his eyes roam about the room, then said without looking at me: "And these paintings, are they real?"

"No," I said.

"Why then do you hang them up?"

"Because I like them," I answered.

He clasped his hands together and gave me a short look, from which I understood my answer did not convince him.

After a long silence, he pointed to a big painting and asked in a defiant tone: "And this painting, what does it mean?"

I inclined my body slightly forward and began to look at it, pretending to show interest. After a long while, I answered: "It means many things."

I said that because I was annoyed that I did not really know what the painting meant and had never tried to know. As I was intently looking at it, I wondered for the first time why I liked it.

# 5

I left the room and went to the kitchen. I was tense and sad. I opened the window and began looking out at the grey roofs and the pigeons perched on them as I tried to soften my sadness. I saw a thin line of smoke rising from one of the chimneys and I continued to look at it until it vanished. In the middle of the buildings, there was a lone sycamore tree. I saw a bird soaring above it, then settling on one of its branches. I thought to myself: "This is another bird whose name I don't know." It was small and had a short beak. I looked at it for a long time, then decided to look up its name in the birds' encyclopaedia that I had bought when I discovered that my knowledge of birds and their kinds was weak.

# 6

When I returned to the room, I found him sitting on the sofa. He gave me a broad smile, so I smiled too. My sadness had vanished. I sat on his chair and leaned my head away to avoid the sunshine. He leaned on a little cushion and stretched his legs, then he put his hands on his knees. I stole a look at the nail of his right-hand little finger. It was long and dirty. I think he noticed my look, for he raised his hand at that moment and scratched his chin.

I looked at the painting he had pointed to, moments ago, and I began searching for what it could mean.

"Your mother says that she received the amount you sent her, and that she repaired the tomb and painted it with lime."

His words surprised me, so I asked, "What tomb?"

"Yourfather's," he answered, still scratching his chin.

I remembered then the letter my mother had sent me several months ago, a long letter written in pencil, in which she criticised me severely and blamed me for neglecting my father's tomb. At that moment, I felt a strong desire to hear her news. But instead of asking him about her, I began to recall her face in my imagination.

7

A dark cloud suddenly hit the sun.

"The weather here changes a lot," he said.

"Yes."

"I believe it's going to rain," he said, looking at the sky.

"Perhaps."

A long while passed during which we said nothing. I remembered that he used to like rain, snails, and tortoises and that he used to swim in brackish water and in the wadi when it overflowed. I began to recall the past, searching for what could help me understand what happened to us later on. I used to like him and he truly loved me. We went to school together and when we obtained the baccalauréat, I joined the College of Medicine because I wanted to become a surgeon but I soon gave up my studies and got lost in the world until I settled in this city by chance. As for him, he was appointed a teacher and I heard, years later, that he had become an important politician in the village and that he was fond of raising chickens.

And here he was now, in front of me, looking at me from moment to moment with eyes whose colour I could not determine. And here I was, digging up that distant past in order to find something to help me bear this human body piled up in front of me.

# 8

He fidgeted a little, then pulled in his legs and sat up.
While I was searching for something to say, he yawned and
stretched his arms, then stood up. I stood up in turn. I did-
n't know why but I suddenly felt I should. He moved toward
a shelf on which old books were heaped: novels mostly by
foreign writers, poetry collections, little encyclopaedias I had
stolen from a library in which I worked.

Tucking the bottom of his shirt in his trousers, he bent over
the shelf, then picked out a book. He read its title aloud and
leafed through it. I came closer to him and said in an enthu-
siastic tone: "It's a wonderful novel . . ." He asked about its
topic, so I related to him its events in an excited manner. He
listened to me silently, then he said, returning the book to its
place: "I don't like war novels."

# 9

It began to rain. We went to the window and looked at the
raindrops running down the dusty glass. A moment later he
asked: "These pigeons, don't they come near your window?"
I said: "Sometimes."

He lit up his pipe and took a long draw on it. Suddenly,
he turned to me and said: "Do you want to send anything to
your mother?"

"Are you leaving now?" I asked in surprise.

He gave me a inquisitive look and said nothing. I remembered at that moment that he used to love me truly and that
I liked him. It occurred to me to invite him to supper but I
did not, out of shame.

Avoiding his look, I said: "No, nothing." Then I added,
confidently: "Tell her I will visit her shortly."

I accompanied him to the door and we said goodbye. I
think he hesitated to shake my hand when I stretched it out
to him. He went down the stairs slowly. I bent over the rail-

ing when he was at a short distance from me and I looked at him as he trudged down the stairs. A moment later, I shouted to him: "Don't forget the stairs are waxed."

I remained motionless, listening to the sound of his heavy footsteps on the wood. When he'd left the building, I returned to my room and lay down on the sofa opposite the painting he had pointed to a short while ago. I looked at it intently, then murmured: "Certainly, it means something."

*Translated by Issa J Boullata*

# The Crop

## GAMAL EL-GHITANI

Before the shadow of the old camphor tree lengthened, before the call to prayer at noon, they stretched out on the ground beside the field when the crop was ripe – a day or two before harvest. The peas had escaped the blight which dries up leaves and drains away the green colour, leaving them like straw. Abd al-Maujud was happy as he looked at his two sons, Jabir the elder, and Abd al-'Al, the younger, and then at the stems of the plants: what remained to be done was not much. The tea hummed in the pot, the only sound in the silence which ruled the day.

The sound of a car, a black car, which slowed down and came to a stop on the road, which was raised a little above the fields. Three men got out, their features indistinct; they looked about them as if searching for something. They stretched out their arms as they descended the slope, their leader ignoring the wet mud. Abd al-Maujud said to himself: "May God bless us!" He thought they were either intelligence agents come to spy on someone or travellers who had lost their way. Their leader was a young man about the same age as Abd al-'Al, a tall man, apparently from Cairo.

"Peace be upon you!"

"And on you, peace and God's mercy and blessing!"

He shook hands, his heart full of welcome. The rough hands gave no sign of fear. Laughing, the young man said: "Perhaps we can sit down!"

Abd al–Maujud said: "Welcome, please do, Sir. Will you have some tea?"

The young man said: "Yes, indeed, father," and asked their names. Then he asked:"Are you the owners of the land?"Abd al–Maujud replied that they were tenants, that the crop was theirs, and that just the crops over there near the water–wheel measured four feddans. One of the other men said that he couldn't tell maize from wheat. Would they forgive him, but was the crop vegetables? Abd al–Maujud told him that all the land in this district was sown with vegetables because it was near Cairo. Tomatoes, onions, potatoes, aubergines, and near the mountain, fruit. Here there were only peas. Yes, (the gentleman sipped the tea from the one metal cup with enjoyment) this is just what he wanted; this meeting, without formality, without an appointment, it was just what he was hoping for; perhaps, God willing, both sides would benefit. Abd al–Maujud replied that it was good that only good would come of it, if God allowed. Then he asked his younger son Abd al-'Al to pick some peas for the gentlemen. The first gentleman laughed. It seemed that Abd al–Maujud knew just what he had come for: he was, he said, employed by one of the new hotels in Egypt, a vast hotel which would open its doors in seven days' time: it would provide food for more than a thousand every day. Though the directors were Western gentlemen, they knew the market and its ways and the tricks of the contractors. They would say: "Why these evasions and detours? We have the farmer; we have the funds; the transport is ready; we have the men in the hotel to lift and carry."

Abd al–Maujud shook his head: "Well, what they have done is fine; it's properly thought out and perfectly organized . . ." At this point they were joined by young Abd al-'Al who, bending down, laid the peas in front of the gentlemen, who tried them. Jabir said: "This is a first–class crop: the pods are full. The traders wouldn't offer these in the market; they would keep them for customers who understood food and its art. But everything has its price." This observation was not lost on the gentleman, who said that the hotel was not so much interested in price as in quality. It was, after all, an international hotel.

Abd al-Maujud was silent. He looked at the other two. One was holding a square black case with a long leather handle. The second seemed to be a partner. He thought he would not expand on the practical details: it was more polite of him to take care of his unexpected guests. He wondered whether the two gentlemen also worked for the hotel. The owner of the black case said that he was a friend of the first gentleman and understood nothing of the hotel business. The other was the driver of the car . . . yes, he worked for the hotel. They were very welcome. Here Jabir broached the subject of selling and buying and enquired as to the sort of quantities the hotel would need. The gentleman replied that the whole crop would be purchased, not only this year but every season – the vegetables, of course. Frowning, Abd al-Maujud said that the land in this district grew nothing but vegetables. All Cairo got its food from here and from the land in the other direction. The land was near the Nile and near the desert. He pointed eastwards where there was no habitation beyond the village: if a camel escaped into the desert, it would be lost and no one would go after it.

The gentleman nodded his head; the driver approved the taste of the peas and asked young Abd al-'Al to pick some for the boss, who said this was impossible, but Abd al-Maujud, hand on heart, said: "A present is not given back." It was only a little thing which the gentleman could take for his children. The gentleman enquired as to the price per kilo. Abd al-Maujud said that they were sold by the sack; the price of a sack was five or six pounds. The gentleman asked: "So how much per kilo?" Young Abd al-'Al looked at his father who said that a sack held about sixty or seventy kilos. The gentleman whistled; he looked at his companion. He seemed to realize something that had been hidden from him. He said that the price in the market was 30 piastres; the excellent variety they were eating now could not go for less than 40 piastres, if it could be found at all. The man with the black case said that he didn't go to the market and knew nothing about prices: "Madame buys everything herself." Abd al-Maujud said that the crops were all around them; that he could find out for himself, and that if there were any other peas like these, then that would be another matter. The gentleman brought the discussion to an end by standing up. The driver stopped and the gentleman with the black case stopped, saying that he would beat about the bush no longer; the price here was very reasonable, the crop excellent, more important still, he felt very well disposed towards Mr . . . Mr . . . Abd al-Maujud. The hotel had found what it was looking for.

Jabir, the older boy, presented a bag of about three kilos to the driver. Young Abd al-'Al asked very earnestly for the address of the hotel in Cairo. The gentleman gestured reassuringly, saying that he would come to them himself after a few days; he would bring special bags for the crop. They would be able to conclude the deal; he would pay cash; there would be no need for them to go to Cairo for payment. They would find it difficult to get into the hotel: in the first place, it was remote, and then there was a constant guard around it. All they had to do was to sign the invoices and receipts.

Abd al-Maujud asked, in an approving tone: "And how would the money reach us?" The gentleman waved his hand. Abd al-Maujud said: "Well, as you please . . ." They would leave it to him and hope that good-will can take care of it all, and make the best arrangement, but wasn't it proper that they should stay for lunch? They made excuses, they thanked him, they wished him well. Abd al-'Al approached the gentleman: wouldn't it be possible to know what day and time to expect them?" The gentleman said that it was not possible to be precise now, but it would be within three days. Abd al-Maujud tried to climb the bank after them, but the gentleman insisted he should stay where he was.

The wheels ground against the earth; the sound gradually died away till silence reigned again. It had all seemed so sudden that Abd al-Maujud asked himself whether he was dreaming or awake. Young Abd al-'Al broke the silence of noon, full of the aroma of crops. He was worried: whatever the business might be, he didn't trust those gentlemen. His father said: "There's no problem at all." He trusted them completely; the gentleman was the soul of honesty and propriety. Didn't he want to have a rest from weariness and disappointment, from loading the crop into sacks, from running to and fro to find someone to share in the hire of a lorry, from going to market on nights when the cold cut into their extremities to sell their crop perhaps all at once, or perhaps when the business was slack, having to go back night after night? Then the waiting for the boss: they couldn't speak directly to him, could only see him at a distance, coming and going in his car, his head wrapped in a white silk kaffiyeh, with his men in front and behind him, one of whom would bring them the bill and the money, and take his share, just as before him, the man standing in front of the scales would do, and the man who directed them to where they should leave their crop – everyone taking or not taking something. Then they would have to find their way home from Cairo. Young Abd al-'Al said that he knew all that, but he still didn't trust the gentleman. Why hadn't he told him the address of the hotel. He would only believe it when he saw lorries coming and money in their hands. Jabir said that he looked like an intelligence officer – intelligence officers usually pretended to be friendly. Abd al-Maujud shouted: "What could intelligence people do here?" Jabir said: "Perhaps they're searching for arms or investigating some track or other." Abd al-Maujud struck the ground with his hand: "Sons, the gentleman asked nothing for himself; he just drank tea with us and enjoyed it." They were silent.

The smell of burnt straw rose in the air. The noon was

heavy, not a branch or leaf stirred. The cobs of maize were fully ripe although there were still a few days of the spring month of Amshir left. At night, Abd al-Maujud said again that he was going to take a rest from the market, its tyranny and wretchedness which had little by little eaten up his life; he was not going to borrow from hither and thither to transport his crops, was not going to scrape together advances from here and there. He didn't want more money, just rest and escape from pain. Next day, before the sun's shadow reached the camphor tree, he raised his head, asking: "Wasn't this the time that the gentleman came?" He did not wait for an answer. He rose, summoning up his courage, his right shoulder a little higher than the other so there was a slight limp in his walk as he climbed the bank. He looked along the empty road, disconcerted. Perhaps they had lost their way. One place in this district looked much like another, and these gentlemen were from Cairo.

The following day he used a palm branch as a stick because he had stood for a long time the day before and his joints were giving him trouble. The time was past when he would raise his hoe and bring it down on the earth from sunrise to sunset. On the seventh day, before sunrise, he became even more disconcerted: had he set too high a price? Had he shown greed? Abd al-'Al told him that he had not been greedy, in fact, had been generous. Perhaps the gentleman had gone to another field; perhaps they had been just amusing themselves during a long journey. He had noticed a smile on the face of the driver.

But Abd al-Maujud paid no attention. After dawn he walked through the fresh dew to the traffic lights. He had instructed the policeman to direct the black car to his fields; perhaps the gentleman was tired of waiting and asking. In the middle of the night he woke up joyfully and described how a strange gentleman he had never seen before had come to him and asked: "Are you Abd al-Maujud?" he had replied: "Yes, Lord." The gentleman had said that the hotel was late in open-

ing because of a lack of customers, but the agreement still
held. The hotel would be late no longer.

Abd al-'Al was almost weeping with despair as he pointed
to the peas drying up and the ruin of the crop. When what
was behind them and in front of them was gone, the Syrian
grapes or the Yemeni figs would then not be within reach.
When the transport van came and the driver from Cairo was
hurrying to load the crop, he approached the man and
enquired about a black car with three young men in it. The
driver laughed, he just laughed.

Abd al-Maujud got up in the middle of the night. Perhaps
the gentleman from the hotel had come: they would take the
crop at the last minute. He did not take his sons with him: for
the first time, he did not go with them. Perhaps the gentleman had come and asked for him. He questioned the people
of the village, asking them, in the name of the Prophet, to
direct a young man dressed in a black shirt who would come
in a black car with a companion carrying a black case, a
square case, definitely square; he asked them to describe to
the gentleman the road to his fields, to describe the old camphor tree, the oldest tree in the whole district. The gentleman
was from Cairo and didn't know the district. He went to the
small shops asking about a black car. He stood in front of
men, he accosted women, he chased small children whom he
suspected of knowing that the gentleman had come and of
concealing it from him. He shouted at every car which flew
past on the road that he didn't care about the night or the
dangers of the road ("There's no blood money when you're
knocked down by a car"); that he would threaten big Jabir
and young Abd al-'Al with his stick; did he want them to lose
the chance of a lifetime? The gentleman had said that he
would come which meant he would come; who knows, perhaps he came in the night. But who would meet him and settle the agreement?

*Translated by Mohammed Shaheen*

# Men have all the Luck

## MOHAMED CHOUKRI

"Always remember you were an abandoned child," she says to me.

"And you? Who are you?" I think of saying to her. "You should remember that I also saved you from your father who divorced that slut of a mother of yours. He was threatening to throw you out of the house if you hadn't married the first person who proposed to you. Everyone says your mother was a slut both before and after she married your father, and today she's a pimp, now that your father's divorced her. Who told you that your father is your real father, then? How can you prove that to me?"

Every time we argue, though. I try to make her understand that her existence and my existence are tied to a man and a woman about whom neither she nor I know the complete truth, because no one is born as he wants to be born, they bring him into the world as they want. By the time a person finds himself able to think about his existence, they've already imposed a life on him to accept or reject in his own way. A human being is a human being, it doesn't matter whose son he is.

She interrupts me, forcefully. "You're an idiot. I've married an idiot. I don't understand you. You're obscene. And don't forget that you're just a foundling."

The pressure builds up in my head. I'm losing the man who can speak to her in my imagination. I beat her and beat her until she faints. Sometimes I fall down beside her exhausted, or I even lose consciousness as well. She usually wakes up several times during the night. She wakes me up insistently:

"Farid!"

"Yes?"

"Get up!"

"Why?"

"Quick, get up!"

"But why?"

"There's someone trying to break into our house!"

"Go to sleep, Yamna! There's no one there."

"Listen to that squeaking!"

"It's the wind shaking the door!"

"Coward! Huh . . . are you a man? You're not a man."

The daughter of a bitch carries on shaking me, kicking me, pulling the blanket off me and hitting me until I get up. Every time I find nothing. Every time, too, I think of throwing myself on top of her and strangling her. In bed, she turns her back on me. The bitch always turns her back on me. I sometimes spend the night staring into the darkness and at the walls. She often shouts in her sleep, or I hear her repeating nonsense. She sometimes turns me out of bed when I want to make love to her, making me hate all women's thighs. Sometimes she cries and brings me back into the bed – when I find an opportunity to kiss her, embrace her, wipe away her tears and make love to her – or else she leaves me to sleep on the hard couch on the floor. Several times, she repeats to me stupidly: "Why am I like this? Why? Why?"

I usually don't know how to explain her situation to her. "Because that's the way you are, Yamna," I say, while at the bottom of my heart I am saying, "Because you are a stupid woman, because you're a member of the revolting human race, Yamna."

Once I didn't want to go back to bed after she had turned me out, so she started screaming: "Get up from there, come here!"

"No. I'm staying here."

"Get up, I'm telling you."

"Why? Didn't you throw me out yourself?"

"You frighten me here, looking like that. You're like a corpse. Get back into bed."

In the eyes of this wretched orphan, then, I am a corpse. I can no longer recall any happy memories with her. In moments of boredom, I think: "Is this the woman I'm going to spend my wretched life with? This woman who only lets me make love to her when she wants to." Even when God allows it, it's difficult and peculiar making love to her. She never opens her thighs. She stretches herself out stiffly. She pulls her thighs tight together as if she were a virgin afraid to be deflowered. For a long time she would not let me kiss her or touch her breasts. "I'm not your whore," she would say to me. "Go and look for a whore to kiss, and fondle her breasts. Respectable people don't do it like that. Hurry up and finish, and get off me. You're too heavy for me, you don't let me breathe properly."

I had great confidence in Doctor Fleuris. As far as I'm concerned, he's a very good young man. Just thinking about him makes me feel calmer. I often go to him with my aches and pains. As soon as I enter his surgery, I feel better. By the time I've come out, my pain has stopped completely, so that sometimes I haven't even bought the medicine. I gave her his telephone number once.

"Take it! This is his telephone number."

"What do you want me to do with this scrap of paper?"

"Don't you know your numbers?"

"It's none of your business whether I know my numbers or not."

God be praised! You created everything. I didn't believe she was so illiterate that she couldn't even read her numbers. She looked at the scrap of paper in her hand. She threw it onto the bed, looked at me then went into the kitchen. "She is a human cow," I said to myself. I was feeling so ill that I had

110

forgotten she was just Yamna the country girl who didn't know what anything was called, or even her numbers. She would appear in front of me then disappear. I imagined her as a young child that had soiled her pretty dress, or an adolescent surprised by her first period who didn't know what to do with herself. "I've married a wretched girl who can't even count her fingers right." 'This . . . that . . . this . . . that . . .,' that's what she calls things when she doesn't know their names. When I want to teach her the name of something, she says to me angrily: "I don't know. I don't need you to teach me."

I screamed, gasping from the depths of my weakness: "Get out, take this piece of paper and ask the local grocer to dial these numbers on the telephone for you. Tell him to ask for Doctor Fleuris for you. He'll come to his shop, then the grocer will bring him to our house. Tell the grocer that I am very ill. Hurry up, go to him. What are you waiting for?"

She began to tremble like me. Her body shook then she burst into tears. She cried and cried until she fell asleep. During the night, I heard her talking wildly in a dream: "Put it all in. Leave it there! Put it all in!"

We reached Feddan Square. Farid was tired but happy. He has great confidence in me. He tells me all the details of his life without the slightest reservation. His masturbation, his wild sex life from which he had been rescued by his marriage to the fair Yamna, and the people who say that her mother was Jewish and her father Moroccan. Before he was married, he used to get on a bus just after twelve o'clock. The bus would be crowded with people at that time. Most of the passengers were students. He would aim for one of the girls' bottoms, rubbing himself against her while the bus was moving until he ejaculated. At night, he would masturbate two or three times, sometimes more. He had lots of naked or halfnaked pictures of singers and actresses and he would masturbate in front of them. I remember Natalie Wood, Elizabeth

Taylor, Sophia Loren, Brigitte Bardot and Marilyn Monroe. He also suffered from a metaphysical fear of death and the day of resurrection. He showed me his watch and said: "What do you think?"

"About what?"

"We'll sell it."

"Good idea."

"He's become like me," I thought. "A few days ago, I also sold my watch in the second-hand market in Tangiers."

We plunged into the crowd in the upper market. I felt a pain in my body. I took a deep breath to relieve my tiredness. I felt sick. I took a sip of water from a cup. Warm water that tasted like snot from a man with a cold. We turned off to the right towards the road that goes through the big garden market. I savoured the smells of the food — fish, bean soup, grilled meat, spices. I savoured them, looking longingly at the dishes displayed in the café windows.

"We'll take our lunch in one of these cafés when we've sold the watch," said Farid. (My mouth was watering and my stomach was desperate for something to eat – either the food I could see or the other dishes whose smells were wafting from the pots over the fire.) We mingled with people buying and selling. Farid gave his watch to an elderly hawker.

"Show it off properly to everyone," he said to him. "I'll pay you more than the basic amount if you show it off properly."

The hawker had some simple things for sale in his hand. "Ten dirhams," he shouted, lifting it up.

"He's got a weak, feeble, hoarse voice," said Farid. "His voice won't attract enough attention from people."

"People will be looking at what's in his hand, not his feeble voice."

"You don't understand much about these things. A strong voice will attract people's attention even if they're asleep."

The bodies around us moved in a sort of limp exasperation. We collided with some of them. Sometimes I felt one of my feet being crushed as another foot squeezed down on it.

Sometimes we would apologise and sometimes we wouldn't. It seemed as though people couldn't find anything to do except to be in this hellish place.

After about half an hour, the hawker sold the watch for 41 dirhams. It was a good watch. Farid gave the hawker four dirhams. The hawker usually took half a dirham for every ten dirhams. At least the wretched man wasn't a pimp.

I felt that I was hungrier than Farid. I imagined a tub of spicy bean soup followed by fried fish and black bread. I imagined myself squeezing half a lemon over the fish. A delicious taste flowed into my mouth. My eyes clouded over. My body shook with longing for food. We went into a small wretched restaurant. A horrid smell wafted from it, mingled with the smell of food and spices. Three people were eating. They looked tired and dirty. They opened their mouths as they chewed. Their teeth were rotten and yellow. They moved their jaws ravenously as they noisily sucked the head and backbone of a fish noisily. They swallowed quickly. One of them had a bad eye. It looked like a black, rotten grape. One of their hands was bandaged up in a rag spattered with blood and filth. Farid avoided looking at them. Their faces looked worn out. All their misery was embodied in their faces. For a moment, I thought of mankind's suffering. I swallowed a mouthful quickly. I had difficulty breathing, so much so that I thought I wouldn't breathe again. Farid came to my aid with a light blow on the back of my head. They looked at me in silence as they gulped down their horrible food. I went back to eating with tired breath. I began to fear every mouthful I swallowed. I got ready to swallow it carefully. I chewed it well and swallowed it slowly. I gripped the side of my seat and pressed my hands on the side before swallowing. Curse this flabby body that I have to put up with! Just thinking about the difficulty of swallowing tortures me before I swallow.

We went into the Continental Café. I still have memories of this café from 1960–61. It no longer has any vitality today.

Cafés become old too. I was sitting in an old café now with Farid, who was almost becoming like the café. Its fresh paint was like powder on the face of a woman living on the memories of her youth. We ordered two beers. Farid's silence signified nothing. It was a dumb silence. When a pretty girl came into the café he would spend a long time eyeing her charms. I don't like him when he tries to mix his worries with mine. When we were studying in al-Ara'ish he would exploit his status as an orphan to beg. I would stand some paces away from him as he approached someone he thought would give him something and begin his act: he would contort his face so that he appeared to be ill and speak in a quiet, feeble voice. When he got something, his personality would change. He would rub his hands together vigorously, his eyes would light up and he would walk about with a swagger, talking self-confidently. What annoyed me about him, the bastard, was when I heard or saw him saying to someone sometimes: "For the two of us, me and my friend there. He is studying with me in the same institute."

I couldn't bear him pointing his finger at me. I would lower my head as well, cringing, and go off with a worried look as he pursued me.

"Why are you so stuck up?", he would say. "We are not doing anything to be ashamed of. We are not begging."

"What are we doing then?"

"We're asking for help because we're two poor students, we're not professional beggars."

We didn't always beg for bread. We smoked, and we liked black coffee and the cinema. Sometimes, we would go to visit some elderly whores. We hadn't received the grant yet. Farid slept with a family who felt sorry for him. The family had two girls who were studying in the institute: one was a consumptive in love with a Moroccan student studying in Syria and the other behaved in an intolerably nervous way. It was with this neurotic that he used to revise maths. The love between them was not well balanced. "She knows that I am

a foundling, Salim," he would say to me. I would spend half
the night in a café whose toilet gave off an odour that stung
the eyes. Sometimes, rats would come out of the hole in the
ground that served as a toilet, wander around in the café then
go back into the hole.

Farid got a mighty shove from Yamna. He was reeling.

"Get out of my sight. Get away from here, you filthy
drunkard!"

His head collided with the wall. He regained consciousness.
I wanted to intervene, but I heard Yamna saying to me: "No,
leave us alone."

"Yes, stay in your place," Farid added.

I saw him curl up under her to grab her legs. His head was
under her breast. She grabbed him by the middle. I laughed
to myself. They were two children, while so far I had been in
control of myself. They fell down. Farid was on top of her,
hitting her.

"My face, my face, you bitch!," I heard him yell, in pain.
"You're scratching me! Right, then, take this!" He aimed a
blow to her face, and the blood flowed from her nose. I heard
Yamna's head bang against the door. Farid got up, staggering
about and panting. "Is this what the bitch wants? Curse the
day I married her!"

He sat down on the bed, exhausted. I said nothing to him.
I watched him in silence. He seemed drained of all will. I felt
my consciousness paralysed. He went into the kitchen and I
heard some mumbling.

"My head . . . Wait! You'll see, you son of a whore!"

He began to sprinkle some water on her face while she
hurled abuse at him.

❧

"In a moment we'll be stopping in Rabat station!" said the
conductor.

Salim stood in the small corridor connecting the two car-
riages. It was the first time he'd ridden in a train. Thousands

of times he had said to himself: "This is the first time. This is the first time I've slept with a woman. This is the first time I've smoked and drunk. I love a girl who's like me. I'm sceptical about life after death. I sleep in the streets like a cat on a wet night. I've got a job. I'm thinking of committing suicide. Friendship is false. Thousands of beginnings of this and that. Some of them finished, some of them unfinished, or still beginning. I felt that the five hours from Tangiers to Rabat were long and boring. I drank a small bottle of wine in the buffet on the train. I smoked a packet of light cigarettes. I saw scenes of fields, farm animals, shepherds and wretched Bedouin. I thought about the Gospel, the Qur'an, Beethoven, Michelangelo and Don Quixote. Possibly this migraine and physical hunger are the result of that bottle of wine. The screeching of the wheels got louder and louder. The train stopped. A young girl hugged an old man. Perhaps I will never have such a feverish wait again in my life. It's enough that I am a son who hates his father. I don't want to hate or be hated."

He stopped a taxi.

"The tourist hotel, please!"

In the hotel, he stared at the dirty marks for a moment, then a horrid smell wafted from the bed, when he drew back one edge of the blanket. Someone must have been having fun on this bed. I lay down. An itching feeling came over me. I imagined bloodsucking insects crawling up my body and wandering over my skin, stopping here and there then biting me and sucking my blood.

He went out to the balcony. He felt like screaming. But for what? The cold night was washing him. Rabat. Tmara quarter. A dirty hotel. Insomnia. Stopping his monthly salary because of some administrative error for which he was not responsible. Lights and loneliness. I am persecuting myself for a reason that I don't understand clearly.

He left the hotel. He stopped a motorcyclist.

"Which way do I go for Mohammed V Street, please?"

"Is that why you're stopping me?"

He left, cursing me. I felt disappointed. I've been packaged like those goods that are dark inside, but bright outside.

He stopped to look at some oranges in a shop window, like sleeping breasts. I am hungry. I like fruit more than meat. The smell of fruit never makes me feel sick. It doesn't drip blood. He stood in front of four or five dogs who were circling around a single bitch. The dogs were sniffing around the hind quarters of the bitch as she ran away. He remembered the last incident, that stopped the traffic in Tangiers for several minutes. The bitch was dripping blood from her vulva. Every drop made a star shape on the ground. The sight amused the children, but annoyed some of the grown-ups who were with their families. The other dogs were running away then coming back.

"Separate them with a good kick," said a man to some youths. No one replied. All the cars were trying to pass carefully, so as not to hurt the suffering pair. Salim thought: "I've often wondered about the agony of copulation between two dogs. My friend Zinati explained it to me once, just like a simple gardener talking about his flowers." Finally, a small hero appeared. With a single kick between the hind quarters of the dog and bitch, the bleeding organs were separated. A long, sharp wail could be heard from them. The youths applauded in admiration at the resolution of the crisis. Salim approached the distressed pair of dogs. The other dogs fled, expecting it to be their turn. That is what the youth had done in the Place de la France. Salim hit hard. A wail, a cry, and the dogs fled. They stayed locked together just as they were. He felt disappointed. I'll try again harder. He aimed his foot, but he felt some weakness stopping his leg from moving.

"For God's sake, Sir, please give me something!" a beggar woman was saying on Goldsmiths Street.

The young lad turned to her. She was holding her baby between her arms. "For my daughter's sake," the woman insisted. "Give me something for the sake of my daughter!"

117

The young lad was standing talking to another youth.

"Say that to whoever it was made you open your legs to get you this daughter of yours!" he said sarcastically.

The woman was astonished and went away sobbing, without saying anything.

After Salim had gone a few steps away, he saw the terrified dogs coming back to hover again around the distressed pair. "Hotel Majestic" he read on the sign on the hotel door.

ॐ

I relaxed. For a moment, I felt that I was my own master, and my tiredness dissolved. I closed my eyes. Things come to me, sometimes, just by thinking about them. I saw one of them in Tangiers taking out some lottery tickets from his pocket. He looked at the list of winning numbers and said to his companion: "Nothing!" Then he looked carefully at the tickets and put them back in his pocket. "If only this number had been here and that number there!" he said to his friend before putting the losing tickets back into his pocket. "My being here now, here in Katie's house, is like the losing lottery tickets that the man put back into his pocket regretfully. My life now is like a losing ticket, but despite that I cling to it. Waiting for what will happen is always less cowardly in my eyes." Katie smokes and drinks beer, looking at the walls and ceiling languidly, without interest. "Tick, tock … tick, tock … ten past seven in the evening, March 1967. Julius Caesar was assassinated in the middle of March, and on the thirtieth several Moroccan citizens died in Tangiers, killed by the bullets of the police of the French Protectorate. I was born in March, so my mother said, though she no longer remembers on which day. I played a game with myself. I wrote the days of the month on some scraps of paper. My hand reached out blindly for one of them. I opened the scrap of paper: 25 March. So I was born on that date. Since then I have no longer been depressed about my lost date of birth. I was born at dawn, so my mother added. Our hands touched blindly but firmly as I chose my birthday from among the scraps of paper. Our hands touched gently, then warmly. I saw my face in miniature in her eyes that were filled with moisture. Her hand became warmer and warmer. The warmth of her body drew me to her. Her hand was moist with sweat. Her light moustache became moist like her hand. With my tongue, I licked the moisture of her light moustache. I smelled the delicious aroma of tobacco in my nose and felt the taste of her mouth on my mouth. She closed her eyes, then opened them like a dying butterfly. She whispered nothing. Silence. Tick tock. I am lost in a timeless space. In a single moment, our bodies were engulfed in a fever. In her eyes there were stars and moisture.

He left Katie's house, carrying his exhaustion into Mohammed V Street. Suddenly, the watchman's daughter confronted him cheerfully. "Salim, you are here!"

He had last seen her on the beach in Tangiers playing tennis.

"But what are you doing here?"

"You can see."

"And your studies?"

She shrugged her shoulders, contracting her face muscles into a scowl. "I got bored with everything in Tangiers and came here to work."

"You're working?"

"Not yet. I am not alone here, I'm with a friend." She pointed to the Paris Arcade shop "She works there. She'll be stopping work in a moment. She is settling the sales accounts now."

Samira appeared, short and plump. Dalila introduced her to him, then hailed a taxi. They got in and Dalila said to the driver: "Brasserie de France café."

When they got out of the taxi, Salim thought: "Their clothes are scruffy. Perhaps they sleep in a seedy hotel like the first hotel I didn't sleep in yesterday." He paid the driver two dirhams and they went into the café.

"It's a month and a half since we left Tangiers. We've begin to get used to our life here, but the problem is that . . ."

"Enough, Dalila," Samira interrupted her. "Don't get agitated. You'll find work too."

"I haven't seen your mother since they moved me to another school," said Salim to Dalila.

The waiter stood in front of them. Dalila ordered a beer, Samira a white coffee, and Salim a beer. "But did your mother agree to you coming here with Samira?"

"I don't let anyone interfere in my life any more. She wore me out with her advice. I couldn't stand her when I realised that she wanted to get rid of me. She told me that she was being courted by a very rich man."

"Be sensible, Dalila. Put on this kaftan. Don't let people hear us arguing. The man will come this evening."

"No, I won't put on this kaftan," she screamed in her face. Put it on yourself. It suits you better than me."

"Be sensible," she said. "You will offer the man and his family some refreshments. Give him the best chance to see your face properly. You are pretty. Be professional when you offer him tea and sweets, be modest. Keep calm. The man is from a well-established Tangiers family, respectable and conservative. Don't shame us in front of respectable people!"

"What does it matter to me that the man comes from an old, conservative, respectable Tangiers family?" I shouted in her face. "No, I'm still young. I'm not sixteen yet. I don't know this man and I don't want to know him. Tell him to look for a proper respectable Tangiers family like his own upper-class lot."

Dalila fell silent. "And did you see the man who wanted to get engaged to you?" I asked her.

"No. I fled in the evening and spent the night at Samira's. In the morning, we came here." Samira put her hands on her knees and smiled from time to time, looking at Dalila with affection and admiration. I looked at Samira with affection too.

120

"She's right," said Samira bitterly. "The same problems were awaiting me. Most fathers are like that now. It's better to get away from them just as soon as we can."

"If I can't find work here, then Samira and I will move to Casablanca," said Dalila calmly. "It's the city for work."

They left the café. A chill breeze wafted lightly over them. Salim stopped a taxi. "Star Cinema," said Dalila to the driver.

Outside the cinema, I realised that several dozen people's eyes were following our movements. It was a men's cinema. I only saw two or three women. I stood between the two of them. I gave Dalila a thousand francs. She was our guide, and she insisted on going to buy the tickets herself. A popular cinema, like the 'Cazar' or 'Capitol' or 'American' in Tangiers.

Samira seemed more serious than Dalila, even though she was the same age or younger than her. Dalila didn't give back the change. I couldn't read the titles of the two films being screened together in the same programme.

Salim was yawning when he heard Samira say to a young man beside her: "If you don't leave me alone, I'll call the police."

Someone stroked Salim's shoulder from behind. "Here you are!" A glass of wine. They drank wine in turns from a single glass here as well, just like in the 'Cazar' and 'Capitol' in Tangiers. I won't refuse a glass. The gunshots and shouts of the Red Indians on the screen sometimes mingled with the shouts of the audience. Dalila prodded me with her elbow. "Here's the second good film beginning."

We left. Tiredness had robed me of all desire.

At first, Salim had wanted Samira. He didn't want Dalila. "Taxi," cried Salim. He no longer wanted to spend the night with them. They lived with two other girls in a single flat. Samira was serious beside him.

"I feel colder in Rabat than in Tangiers," said Dalila. Salim noticed a movement in Samira's legs: she was brown skinned, with a face as round as an apple, chestnut coloured hair, and breasts like eggs.

The two girls got out of the taxi and he continued on his way to his hotel. The streets were deserted. "Rabat nights are different from Tangiers nights," he thought. "There, there would be people out visiting the Boulevard and the inside market now."

He always liked the sun in the morning. He hadn't slept well. He was walking along, people's faces passing before him like trees seen through the window of a speeding car. Tireder faces than those he was used to seeing in the cities in the North. I'm here, crushed in this city that I'm visiting for the first time. "Which do you like best, sunset or sunrise?" he had asked his friend Karima in the Picnics Bar one early morning.

She was astonished. "I've never thought of the sunrise or sunset before," she replied, like a puzzled child.

"Try," he said. "Tell me later which is the more beautiful."

He met her several times and repeated the same question to her as a joke. Every time, she answered him quite seriously: "One day I'll try."

"Start this evening," he would say to her. "I'll give you a nice present if you try."

"Not today. One day I'll try. I don't like people who tell me what to do."

He saw Samira in the distance arranging clothes on the sales cart in front of the arcade. They greeted each other, then he said to her: "I'm going back to Tangiers."

"Won't you stay with us one more day?"

"I can't, I'm working tomorrow." She put her finger to her temple. "I was going to say something important to you," she said. "But what was it? I'm often forgetting these days. Ah, I remember! Don't tell Dalila's mother that you saw us here. Come back to us one day!"

"And where is Dalila now?"

"I left her sleeping."

He smiled at her and said goodbye. She waved her hand. He remembered his friend Aziz who had said to him one day: "Sometimes, to feel true love means to be travelling in a train,

122

while your loved one travels in another train in a different direction." He turned towards her one last time; her smile seemed sad.

I also realised she wasn't happy about the baby but that she didn't want to stop it growing inside her. "Have an abortion, if you don't want it," I said to her. "No," she said. "Do you want to cast me into hell? No, do you think I am like you? I am not a criminal."

The unborn child was imposing itself on us day by day. It was growing, while I was telling myself: "Yet another problem! Its screams will fill the house in what should be its calm and peaceful moments. It will be no different from all the other annoying children in the world. How I hate the screaming of babies! Still, I know that screaming is all a child can do to express himself."

A week after the birth, I came across a scrap of paper written in a childish hand. The letters had no dots, and the lines were slanting. I showed her the scrap of paper. She threw it away and started to tremble. "Take it away from me. Where did you find it?"

I snatched it back. "I found it slipped inside *The Entertainer*."

"Get it out of the house. No, keep it. We'll look for someone to cancel its effect. A sorcerer's work can only be cancelled out by a sorcerer as powerful as the first one."

Clutching the child to her, she started to weep. She was kissing him and stroking his head affectionately. "A curse on all envious women! A curse on me as well! I wish I had been born a man! You men have all the luck. It's us women that bear your burdens!"

After some effort, full of nausea and uncertainty, I gathered from her that some childless woman must have laid this spell for her to make her sterile and take her fertility from her. I made her understand that it was only a chapter of the Qur'an, written in a confused way and full of mistakes, and that fertility and sterility had no connection with magic. But her delusions were deep-rooted. She took some money and went off to look for a powerful sorcerer who could cancel out the effect of the spell. "A sorcerer's work can only be cancelled out by a sorcerer as powerful as the first one," she kept repeating to me, tense and fearful.

"Farid!"

"Yes!"

"Get up!"

"Why?"

"There are demons wrestling in my soul. Curse me for marrying a man like you, afraid of his own shadow!"

After the shock of the spell, she began to suffer from serious nervous attacks. She would ask forgiveness for imaginary sins she had not committed. "What have I done, Lord? I am innocent. They wish me ill. Save me from them. You alone know well what is wrong with me!"

"Farid!"

"Yes!"

"Recite a chapter of the Qur'an for my sake. Reciting the Qur'an will lessen my woes. Recite a chapter to me. I am so miserable!"

I recited her a chapter or two. After I finished, I asked her: "And now?"

"I feel better now."

Her high-pitched crying would continue on and off for hours, mingled with the screaming of the child. I've married a sick, stupid woman, I thought. I'll no doubt end up sick and stupid like her. Even the child wasn't wanted by either of us. What exactly made me marry her? I don't know. I must have been out of my mind, in despair of waiting to find the girl I dreamt of, hating masturbation. Sex! This is my problem, Salim! Sometimes we would come to blows as the child screamed. Once I shouted in her face: "Enough! You've won!"

We confronted each other. We were both panting, miserably, stupidly. "Do you want us to go on?" her looks said to me. "No! I've told you you've won!" I imagined myself replying.

I divorced her. This was the only solution for her. Her father came to see me. I was out of the house, watching Muhammad Ali Clay beating his English opponent on the television in the café. I found her father waiting for me in front of the house. He told me that we would talk. When we had gone inside, I asked him to sit down but he refused. I could see evil in his eyes. "Why did you hit my daughter?" he asked. "Speak, you bastard. Speak!"

He didn't wait for me to explain. He threw himself on me and we started to exchange violent blows in this very room. He was biting me and cursing me in that peasant accent of his that I couldn't understand. When we were tired out, we collapsed onto the bed and he started speaking to me:

"I'll kill you, you bastard! You don't know yet what country people are! I saw the evil in your eyes the first day you came to ask for my daughter in marriage. A lot of people told me I'd be mad to give my daughter in marriage to a bastard like you. Everyone knows that you're a foundling who grew up in an orphanage. God wouldn't be happy with this relationship. But I took pity on you. I told them it didn't matter. It's enough that he's a man who wants to be like everyone else. He is a Muslim and a Moroccan citizen. Some one told me that your mother didn't have any fixed religion. I didn't believe it, but today I believe everything that's said about you, you animal! You ruined my daughter's upbringing, then divorced her to wander around in the streets.

Women and children had gathered at the door. A red foam was streaming from his mouth. I had scratches on my face and neck and bites on my shoulder, arms and back. Some of his bites had pulled off my skin. He tried to grab the bottom of my stomach. I was saved by a head butt that I gave him in his face. As he staggered around, I gave him two blows in the stomach. He curled up, then sank onto the ground.

"Yamna, where is she now?"

"I don't know. Perhaps she's in her father's house or whoring somewhere."

"And the child?"

"I've given her responsibility for him."

Farid was talking in a tired voice. He had a dreadful pain in his stomach. He bared his abdomen, which was covered in blotches. The spots were coffee-coloured. "What's this?" I asked him in astonishment.

"That's another story. I was sick. My neighbour, Qadiri, came to visit me with a faqih. I explained to them that I didn't believe in quack remedies from faqihs. Qadiri got angry, regarding my words as an insult to him and to the faqih who was with him. They looked at each other in silence for a moment. "What do you want from me?" I thought. Suddenly they laid into me and tied my hands behind my back with a piece of rope. I began to scream. They gagged me. Yamna brought a brazier from which sparks were flying. The bastard faqih proceeded to heat a skewer until it was red hot, then started to cauterise my stomach, spitting on my burns. Meanwhile, the smell from my skin was making me choke, and I started to vomit through my nose and wet my pants. He was cauterising me with an intoxication that I could see in his fox-like eyes. He was reciting some secret text while Qadiri, the pimp, nodded his head in time. "Carry on, with God's blessing. Everything is going fine," I heard him say to him.

"He's really ready for treatment," said the fox.

My head was filled with a mad screaming. My heart was beating fast. I heard Qadiri say to me: "Have some sense, Mister Farid. Just a few moments, and everything will turn out okay. You are in the presence of a man whose blessing is better than treatment by a thousand doctors. Oh! If only you knew who you were with now!"

The quack continued calmly branding my stomach. I tried unsuccessfully to escape from Qadiri, who was holding me as tightly as possible, despite the fact that my wrists were tied behind my back.

"A little patience. Curse the Devil and calm down! Let us save your life. God is our witness that we are not harming you at all!"

"Help, help!" I imagined myself screaming.

"We understand your position. We are not blaming you, Mister Farid. Be sensible. You're with the best of men. His blessing is a gift from God and from God's true saints."

The quack finished the treatment. Qadiri untied the gag on my mouth. "I'll kill both of you later," I said weakly.

"It's disgraceful to speak such words in front of this good man," said Qadiri. "It doesn't matter to me that you insult me, but you must respect this distinguished man."

He released my hands. I directed a kick at the quack, who had come nearer to me, but it didn't hit him, the bastard. "Curse you both!" I said feebly.

"Goodness me, Mr Farid," said Qadiri. "You weren't like this before."

My head was spinning. I was breathing with difficulty. I wanted to spit on them, but I was afraid they would think me in need of still harsher treatment than the treatment they had already given me.

I went to visit Doctor Fleuris. He prescribed a tonic for my depressed nervous state and some ointment for the burns on my stomach that had turned septic.

They left the Rebertito Bar. "You must stop your habit before you collapse again," said Salim.

"You know that I am afraid of the clap. I used to masturbate once or twice a week even when I was married to Yamna. And when I was making love to her, I used to imagine another woman. Who could marry Yamna and not masturbate?"

"Do you know who runs this house?" Salim asked him, pointing to the house they were approaching.

"No."

"Let's go up. Perhaps she is still here."

"Who?"

"Madame Shama. I know her."

Lalla Shama opened the door to them. "I thought that you would still be here, Lalla Shama!" said Salim.

"Where do you want me to go?"she asked him.

She shook hands with us and asked me: "And you, are you still in Tangiers?"

"Yes."

"And the 'inner' market is still a haven for hippies?"

"Where do you want them to go?"

"Even here in Tetouan, they have begun to invade us in quantities like locusts. They live in the suburbs and the poor quarters."

"They like simple living."

"But they are dirty. The girls are giving our young men the clap."

"They are not all diseased, Lalla Shama!"

"They are very dirty. The men and the women alike. Dirt causes disease. A woman who sleeps with a man and doesn't wash inevitably gets sick and passes the infection to anyone who sleeps with her."

"That's true."

Madame Shama seemed happy, as usual. A girl appeared there, standing, smoking. She turned towards them coldly. Farid left Salim to make an arrangement with Madame Shama and went a few paces away from them. "There's another girl busy with a man," said Salim to Farid. "You go with this one and I'll wait for the other one."

"You go in first," said Farid. "I'll wait for the other one."

"It's all the same to me, but you go with this one if you want. She's attractive, don't you think?"

"It's better you go first."

"Okay, let's toss a coin for it. Whoever wins, goes in first."

Madame Shama laughed. The girl jumped up from her place and went over to them. Madame Shama looked at the girl. "They're going to toss for you," she said. It's the first time I've ever seen this in my life."

Salim tossed the coin in the air. He caught it and covered it, with his right palm on top of the back of his left hand. "Heads or tails?" he asked Farid.

Farid smiled and hesitated. "Tails," he said.

Salim lifted his hand. "Heads."

"Give me a bottle of beer," said Farid to the Madame. He fell onto the chair. Salim followed the girl to her room. She had a smile that reminded him of an Irish girl he had known in Tangiers.

"Your friend seems worried."

"That's the way he is."

Madame Shama came in carrying a tray with two beers on it. "Hasn't the girl my friend's waiting for come out yet?" asked Salim.

"I heard the door to her room opening. The man who went in with her is getting ready to leave."

Salim thought of his friend Salwa. Perhaps I'll find that she's gone back to Tangiers. She likes cold beer and Lucky Strike cigarettes. I once heard her say to her friend Afaf: "I perk up and put on weight when I spend the spring in Meknes and the winter in Marrakesh, but in Tangiers I lose weight all the time."

Salwa's life depended on the health of her cunt.

She handed him his glass. "Your mind seems to be elsewhere."

He smiled at her. "Sorry, I'm like that sometimes."

He looked at her smile, the movement of her lips and her head. "She's nice," he thought. She drank her glass and began to take her clothes off. I have to rid myself of joy and sorrow as easily as she is taking off her clothes. How I wanted to stop what happened to Salwa with that merchant.

"How much is this skirt?" she asked

"I don't sell to drunkards in the morning. It brings me bad luck. Get out of my shop."

"I'm buying from you. It doesn't matter to you whether I'm drunk or not. Tell me how much!"

"Get out!"

"Once a fishmonger, always a fishmonger. From fishmongers in al-'Ara'ish to clothes sellers in Tangiers, they all despise their customers."

"Get out of my shop!"

"I won't get out! Tell me the price of this skirt so that I can take it!"

"Take it then!"

He punched her hard. None of the bystanders intervened. I wanted to intervene. One of them said to me: "Stay where you are! Don't interfere in what doesn't concern you. Are you her keeper?"

They were encouraging the shopkeeper to carry on hitting her. "Give it to her!""More!""She deserves more than that!" "He's a respectable, god-fearing man!" "Drunken whore!" "We'll give evidence on his behalf!"

Her nose was bleeding. "You see! This wretched daughter of a bitch has come and harassed me quite often enough. I told her 'I don't deal with drunkards', but she behaved with me like a bitch on heat. She abused me and all my family!"

"Yes, you are right. We're on your side."

"She sleeps with Europeans in the Boulevard hotels," one of them said. "I know some Christians that she goes with."

"It's true, she's a bitch!"

"No one even knows where she came from."

"She's more of a whore than a chicken," as the Spanish say. A policeman appeared. "Take her away," he said roughly. "That's what she's like, the stinking woman."

Everyone shrank from picking her up. She was lying on the ground, her eyes open, her nose streaming with blood and snot, and her clothes torn. "Take her away. She's playing her usual game with us."

Two people lifted her up under her arms. Her head swung forward. When they got near the police station an elderly drunk sneered at the policemen: "Get back! You know who she is! You saw what happened to her. What are you waiting for now? Go and look for something else."

Salim began to come on top of her. He thought of the 'The Naked Maja' by Goya and felt weightless. The disgusting slimy mouth opening and closing and sucking his thing.

When he left the room with the girl, he saw Madame Shama looking upset.

"Your friend left with the girl he went in with," she said. He was surprised. "How did that happen?" he asked her.

"Ask him. I don't understand what happened either.

"Did poor Yamna go with him?" the girl asked Madame Shama gently.

"Yes," said Lalla Shama sarcastically, pointing at Salim. "She went with him. Tell Salim to take you with him as well if he wants to."

The girl laughed as she looked at Salim affectionately. He sat on a chair and asked Madame Shama for a beer.

*Translated by Paul Starkey*

# A Plait for Maryam

## SAID AL-KAFRAWI

"By the way, the old days were better."

She said that and left the bedroom. She collected up the dirty clothes and threw them on the bathroom floor by the washing-machine. He was lying in bed, his eyes closed, his hand on his forehead; he could just hear the children in Taiba school singing.

"Get up, love, it's almost noon." Startled, he opened his eyes and leaned back against the Arabesque bed head and replied: "Good morning." He had a bitter taste in his mouth and was careful not to swallow his saliva.

She stood by the door, tightening her dressing gown with a leather belt. He looked at the shining buckle and said to himself, "Goodness me! That's my belt!" She rummaged around in a small sideboard of silver ornaments, and opened up an ivory box; she took out a small photograph and stared at it. Then she remarked: "Have you noticed that men seem to get shorter as they get older." Crossing the room to him barefoot, she added: "Look, love, in this photograph you looked taller. Now you have shrunk a little."

He watched her through the mirror as she pursed her lips and took a long look at herself. He saw her nervously pulling out a white hair. Then she called out to him: "Do you think a woman would be better off dying her hair?" Before he could answer, she gave a long laugh. It resonated in the empty flat; its echo splintered his heart. It was going to be a disagreeable morning, like all those he seemed to be experiencing lately. He got up, left his bed and walked over to the empty space between the cupboard and the bed. His body rubbed against hers. He gave her a sympathetic pat and said:

"Look, love, all of us grow old; no one is satisfied."

He crossed the hallway and went to the balcony. His eye caught the painting by Rizq-Allah which was called "Clean limbs in the light". He was dazzled by the glowing bright red colours of the limbs lit up by the rays of the sun in the background. He looked out onto the street. It was empty; dust whirlwinds of Autumn hitting the house fronts and the dark branches of bare trees mercilessly beseeching upward to the skies.

"Are you going to stand there for long? Come in and do something. Help me!"

He came back in the flat and his eyes took a while to get used to the dimness inside: "What's the matter, love?"

He lit a cigarette and sat in the armchair opposite his desk and pondered about his life. What passed now seemed quite surreal and filled with questions. He noticed that whenever he watched her closely, trying to understand what she meant, he would catch her staring back at him questioningly.

She stood in front of him holding the naked lady statue and gazing intensely at him. He feared she might hit him on the head with it. Then she said: "Do you remember where we bought this?"

"Of course."

"Of course? I bet you don't. You're already starting to forget names."

He resented her constant nagging, and he could not stand how she behaved during the night, when he would wake to find her not there beside him. He would get up and look for her in the closed rooms. He would hear her broken sobs coming from the balcony. He would go to her, take her hand and gently stroke her hair.

He heard her cleaning the shutters and singing an old song.

133

She stopped and said: "Don't you get bored in this prison you've put yourself in?"

"Love, the country's changed and things aren't what they used to be. Times change and we all get old."

"Then you are making me older before my time."

He noticed how lately things had become confusing for her and her behaviour perplexed him. She had banned him from walking about the flat at night. When he asked why, she had answered: "Because it's filled with bad dreams."

She turned her attention back to pulling out her white hairs.

He turned the radio on and the Andalusian music carried him back to his childhood. He remembered his mother and her final days when he would take her to the river at sunset and she would automatically turn round and go back home. When he asked her where she was going, she would answer, "Home my son, can't you see it is getting dark?"

His wife said: "Didn't I read yesterday the story of Anna Maria Simone?"

"Dead boring, but a great story."

"A pity! That woman lived a seductive life of lies."

"The important thing, love, is how the story is written."

"What do you mean how a story is written? The important thing is the unforgettable pain."

"That's true." She stared at him for a while and then added: "Does it always have to end with the heroine climbing up onto a chair and her body dangling from a rope!"

She mimicked this by pressing on her neck and hanging her tongue out like someone who had been strangled.

He swallowed hard and felt a great pain in his chest. And he remembered the story from his childhood of a fisherman who had lost his son at sea and waited for him all his life. The father had continued to hear the boy's crying from the waters until the end of his days.

She brought out the electric fire and turned it on.

He said: "It's not cold yet!"

She moved away and picked up a small harmonica that was on the desk, starting to play a well-known tune mixed up with another, sad melody. She threw down the harmonica and walked towards him, an expectant look on her beautiful face.

"It's possible?"

"What's possible?"

She turned her back to him, and went over to the fire. A moment passed before she suddenly grabbed the red-hot bar, and then clenched her teeth in soundless pain. He jumped up in alarm and screamed: "What on earth are you doing?" He put his arms around her and heard himself calming her, despite his urge to scream out: "And this is what it's come to? . . . We have to bear it."

They walked together in the darkened flat, the blinds pulled down. She rested her head on his shoulders and could cry no tears. He woke in the morning to the sounds of the wind beating against the shutters. Filtering through were the songs of school children and the commanding voice of the gym teacher giving them their morning drill.

"Attention, Third Grade! Forward march! Stop! Stay in line! Forward march!" Then the repetitive sound of the drum . . . troom troom . . . troom . . . troom troom . . . troom. And he could just hear the children going up the school stairs while the loudspeaker was broadcasting national songs.

He felt the bed empty beside him. It was cold. He got up to look for her as always. When he did not find her inside, he went out onto the balcony. She was sitting hunched up in the bamboo chair, her hands clenched, one palm wrapped in white gauze. She stared at him with her eyes full of tears. Her thick black hair had been shaved to the scalp.

*Translated by Mona Zaki*

# *Bad Soup!*

## L A T I F A   B A Q A

Last night's soup was very bad. I thought of telling Fatima about it before leaving the house; she might make better soup next time around. I quickly put on my coat and burst out of the door, almost treading on the child. I bang the door behind me; the child is crying.

My eyes slam into the sun outside. At the bus-station, the sunrays are slowly petting the faces. The bus arrives at last, crawling under the weight of a people of a certain type, all of whom agree that it is Monday – the beginning of a new week.

"Ouch!"I scream; someone has trampled on my foot.What a morning! I'll start with the lady who owns the electric appliances store. She's promised to look into the matter, and to receive me at 9.00 a.m.

I stand in front of the shop window to quickly tidy my dishevelled hair ruffled by the bus passengers. Everything is in good order!

"I have an appointment with the lady who owns this store. She said she'd receive me at 9 o'clock." (I glance at my plastic watch; it is 9.00 am sharp.)

The doorman is fat and unfriendly, "Madame is not here!" he says.

"But she's promised to help me, and she gave me an appointment at . . ."

"Come back in an hour," he says, cutting me short.

The thought of going for a walk around town to discover its morning crosses my mind. I burst out laughing – What morning and what evening! What a lousy day! I remember my cousin who is a "zeffat"in Lille – France. "Zeffat" means that he returns to Morocco in the summer, clad in an old suit, ironed immaculately to hide any traces of its former French owner, and that he brings cheap presents for all the members of the family. My cousin cannot stop talking about France, what a paradise it is, and how life there is a dream made real. "There are plenty of jobs," he would say. "The salary you get is in proportion to the work you do; work is available in abundance; you can work twenty hours a day if you so wish; you're paid full salary up to the last minute you have worked; just picture with me …"

But who is spoiling my stroll around the city? I glance at him; a silly smile animates his face. I stop and start walking the other way. He does not say anything. He looks like the boy who, along with the other boys, was involved in the "rape" of Si al-Hadj's she-ass. Poor guy! His looks, which appeared so insolent just a moment ago, are now gradually fading away before the now derisive impression glistening in my eyes.

"Haven't you found any other she-ass to rape, except Si al-Hadj's?" I ask him, keeling over with laughter.

Si al-Hadj is the tribal leader. He owns a black she-ass with bright eyes. It was harvest season; when the men went out to the fields, the wretched youngsters had already decided on their programme for the evening.

In her eye-witness account of the she-ass scene, Aisha, the snub-nosed little girl, said that when the boys were penetrating the animal with their little things, the she-ass was grinning and its eyes were brighter than usual. Later on, Mmi Iada, who enjoys these kinds of things, related that there was a very strange glow in the animal's eyes. Every time she walked past a group of men who included Si al-Hadj among them, the owner of the she-ass, Mmi Iada would say: "Some problems are of my own making; others are caused for me by my she-ass."

Enraged, Si al-Hadj would heap words of abuse on her: "Away with you, ugly crone!"

Still strolling, I walk by a bookshop window where I see many books that I haven't read yet. I remember the hungry character in *Days of Lentils*. He would walk into a bookstore, purchase all the books he wanted and leave.

Can I do the same? I go straight to the shelves on the right: History books, novels, science books, and books on religion. I turn to the opposite side: science books in all fields. I pick up a book by Barthes, a copy of which I had seen in the window of the bookstore. I read the back cover. My big handbag is open.

"I'll just let the book slide quietly into the handbag. I look at the cashier. He's busy with one of the customers. No problem at all. This is great! Ah, the upper floor! Why is that guy looking at me? He's smiling too?"

I pretend to be busy in the hope that he will get bored and look the other way. At that very moment, the bookshop assistant walks toward me and asks me if I am planning to purchase the book. I raise my head and level a glance at the man on the upper floor. I return the book to its place and storm out of the bookstore.

"Is Madame back?"

The doorman flings me a scornful look as if he owns the place and says that she is not.

"Even though it's half past ten!" I remark.

"I said Madame is not here yet. She may not come at all. Besides, we have no vacancies. We have two cleaners who do the daily cleaning."

Daily cleaning! What's there to explain to this Devil? Shall I tell him what Madame told me? Shall I tell him that I'm fed up with the soup of my brother's wife and of the screams of the brood which my brother and she have begotten over a period of nine years at a rate of one child a year? Or shall I

138

inform him that I didn't come here to be a cleaner, that I am clean, that the situation has become unbearable for me, and that I hold a BA in that fantasy they call 'sociology'? The fat doorman is busy with some clients.

"Come back tomorrow!" he says.

"I certainly will! I'll ask my boss at the bakery for yet another morning off. And I might find Madame in her office!"

At home, I forget to tell Fatima what I thought about last night's soup, that was no different from all other the soups she has made. What is this idea of mine that she should improve her soups, which has been growing in my mind since I don't know when?

My brother does not notice the soup is bad; that the screams of his pack of children are getting worse; that the price of his cigarettes has increased threefold in two years; that he hasn't laughed in a long time. Fatima, who finds all this quite natural, never stops peeling carrots and turnips, to make soup every night. What about me, what is it exactly that I want to change? Is it the fact that I work at a modern bakery for a monthly salary of three hundred dirhams? Ah, I remember! There is my cousin, the Zeffat, who has spoken to Fatima about his wish to get hitched to me, in spite of what has been said about me and my being thirty-one years old, of what he has heard about my "masculinity" and my immeasurable self-conceit. My cousin also says that he will return to the country once and for all for this very purpose, that he will rent a house for us, and that I won't have to work.

"This is the solution!" he says. "You'll be the lady of the house, just like all married women. You'll sweep the floor, wash clothes, have children – "the most important thing is to be able to procreate, so that he won't reconsider the matter" – and cook."

Cook! Cook soup every day! The kind of soup that Fatima makes?

"Fatima, your soup last night was horrible!" I scream.

"Really!" she says, "So what! Your brother gulps anything."

139

My cousin would be ready to swallow anything, too: soup, the increase of the price of sugar, bread and cigarettes, and the never-ending screams of kids.

"To hell with you, my bald cousin!" I shout.

My shout startles Fatima, who is sitting beside me changing her son's clothes.

"What! What! What did you say?" she asks.

"Nothing! Nothing at all."

*Translated by Ali Azeriah*

# *If She Comes*

## TAYEB SALIH

"International Bureau of Tourism Arts" the three-by-two-metre oak sign boldly declared. The letters were in huge gilt thulth[1] calligraphy on a green background, and the frame was painted yellow. The sign was hung on the third floor of a decaying building. Amin, not someone who withholds things on his mind, blurted out the first thought that came to him that morning.

"I don't believe in cheap advertising," he said as he stared at the ceiling of the office. "International Bureau of Tourism Arts? Are we running a cabaret, or selling booze?" The ceiling could use a coat of a bright colour.

Without the least intention of enticing her colleague, Sana' slowly raised her luxuriant eyelashes. "Amin, you're one of those naïve and obsessive perfectionists."

For the first time that morning, Amin gave her a good look. A deliberate and fixed stare, in fact. Sana' was not his type. She drove to the office in a sharp 1949 Foxwell. She was spoiled – the daughter of a company director – and had failed her college second-year tests three times before dropping out of her own choice. Had she wanted to stay, nobody would have stopped her.

"When we over-advertise a product, we trigger people's instinctive distrust," Amin finally said, feeling a twitch in his

---

1 thulth is an elaborate style of Arabic calligraphy used usually for decorating mosques with Qur'anic verses

eyelid from the constant gaze. "It's like awakening their defense mechanism. The subconscious protects consumers from slip-ups."

Amin has read some Freud and he liked to insert the subconscious into conversations.

Unconsciously Sana' touched her earrings. They were long crescents dangling from silver chains. She was generous with her make-up, especially the red lipstick, and the scent of her perfume was everywhere. Her dresses were made of silk and their sensual swish with every move made you aware of her voluptuous body. She was not his type, true, possibly even a bit vulgar, but Amin thought Sana' had something that kept attracting him. He was opening his mouth to speak when Baha' walked in.

"You look like an idiot with your mouth wide open," Baha' said, harshly but playfully. "Have I just caught you flirting with Sana'?"

Sana' laughed and rose from her seat, then sat down when she realized she had no reason to get up in the first place. Baha', Amin felt, was conceited and when he wanted to curse him by comparing him to a Hollywood actor, he couldn't recall a single name. He dropped the whole idea.

Baha' sat down behind his desk and blew on its glass surface. There was no dust there, but he did this every morning as if to prime his energy for work. He put his leather case on the desk, patted its side gently, and then opened it. He brought out notebooks, sheets of paper and tourist flyers.

"I stopped by Cook's on my way here and they gave me these," he explained as he scattered the flyers on the table. "Even better, I coaxed a Swedish woman into meeting me tonight."

Sana' hemmed. She knew she needed to better control her reactions.

"Harrods," Amin said after a period of silence.

"What?" Sana' inquired.

"Harrods. H A R R O D S," Amin said. "A department

store in London. How I wish I could go to London and buy a woollen jacket from Harrods!"

"My goodness! By God!" Baha' finally said. He rose from his chair and turned on the air conditioner, and at once the lifeless room was suffused with a dull buzz. An air conditioner, a new green telephone, and a bookcase with glass doors stuffed with sundry books: volume seven of the Encyclopedia Britannica; *Al-Mustatraf fi kul fan Mustadhraf*; a book on international law by someone named Lillienthal; *Teach Yourself Spanish in Seven Days*; Rihlat Ibn Battuta[3]. And who was rubbing knees with the medieval traveller but Lucretia Borgia. And a volume of the telephone directory, and on a discreet corner of the bookcase the *Woman of Rome* next to Mustafa Sadiq al-Rafi'i[4]. No surprise, then, in the coupling of Said Aql's[5] *Randali* with Bernard Shaw's *Mrs Warren's Profession*.

With nothing to do, Amin kept staring ahead till his eyes landed on the lower part of Sana's body, visible from below her desk top. She sat right across from him and when she crossed her legs he shivered. He diverted his gaze to a big map of the world on the wall, but only for a second, then steered it back, cautiously, as though he were driving on a rugged mountain road. And he looked. He felt a tiny twitch between his shoulders but nevertheless traced the thigh from the knee to where it disappears in the folds of the dress. The smell of wet clay tickled his nose, and a wayward thought hit him. Her thigh was white, her arms red and her neck tan.

Sana' stretched her upper body in tempting relaxation. She looked at Amin and her lips parted a little without smiling. Was she vulgar, Amin wondered again. Probably easy to get. Dumb, highly impressionable and someone who tried to

---

2 [*The most Fascinating Topics from every Elegant Art*] was compiled by Egyptian Shihabudin Ahmed Al-Abshihi in the 15th century and is today the only traditional Arabic encyclopedia still printed, distributed and read.
3 [*The Travels of Ibn Battuta*] chronicles the remarkable travels of Ibn Battuta (1304–1369) over about 30 years
4 Mustafa Sadiq al-Rafi'i (1880-1937) was a writer from Egypt
5 Said Aql is a prominent Lebanese poet

relive the European fiction she read. Perhaps she had read *Lady Chatterley's Lover* last night and gone out looking for a peasant.

He was indeed harsh in judging her since at that very moment Baha' was wondering why Sana' liked others to think she was accessible. He remembered too well the night of his disappointment when he asked her out for dinner. She accepted immediately – and how deceived he was with that acceptance. They had a very enjoyable dinner at a restaurant; he was funny and she kept laughing under the guardianship of Eros. Utterly and mutually enjoyable. They left for a ride in a car he borrowed from a friend and drove along a quiet road by the sea. The darkness was soft and dense but you could hear the waves rolling onto the beach.

"I like darkness and rain and the desert," Baha' said in a quivering voice. "Winter is my favorite season, and I loathe spring. Yes, spring's a hateful season." Before his eyes floated images of velvety arms being caressed.

Not bad, Sana' thought, from a man who wasn't exactly poetic. Baha' was baffled by her lack of response. Why was she keeping this respectful distance? Perhaps she was faking it? He stretched out his hand and touched hers. She sat still – didn't move her hand, yell at him, or come closer. Her hand laid there lifeless as if separate from herself.

Baha' continued holding the steering wheel with one hand and working on the dead hand with the other. It was futile and he felt mortified and stupid and so he withdrew his hand.

"Should we go back?" he offered.

"I think we'd better," she said.

When he went to bed that night, he consoled himself with the thought that failure was an experience in itself and promised himself to steer away from those virtuous women who displayed a playful exterior. You get nowhere with them.

The sarcastic smile on Baha's lips certainly eluded Amin. He was talking about Harrods and he wanted to proceed. "Harrods," he ventured after clearing his throat.

Baha' was writing something. He stopped, put the pen aside and looked at Amin for a few seconds.

"What about Harrods?" he said impatiently.

"It's a store in London."

"I know that," Baha' raised his voice. "In Knightsbridge. I have read about London, too. But what's your point?"

"The point," Amin said, also raising his voice, "is that I don't like the name of our agency. It's cheap. I believe in meaningful advertising – intelligent advertising that acknowledges the thoughtfulness of its patrons. Like that at Harrods."

"Harrods is one thing and we're another. We didn't exactly choose the name to please literary critics. It's just a name. What's in a name, anyway?

Amin was silent but not convinced. Baha', he thought, was cheeky and liked to dominate others. Perhaps his dad had been too harsh with him when he was growing up. He appointed himself manager of the agency, made decisions, signed papers and put the company's bank account in his own name. Amin's resentment raged a little and then subsided when it struck him that the International Bureau of Tourism Arts during its whole month of existence had yet to take on a single client. For the agency's owners, the bank account was no more than a gesture of hope in some future and for the bank a mere show of goodwill.

Suddenly something happened that took him out of his thoughts. Something that transformed that decrepit office space with its faded walls, worn carpet, air conditioner and sundry books into a workplace with a purpose. In that flash of an instant, life suddenly seemed good and proved that not all hopes were mere illusions. The phone finally rang.

Sana' jumped and Amin's mouth dropped, but Baha''s hand, an emblem of sheer determination, reached out and lifted the receiver. He brushed his hair with his hand and cleared his voice to produce, from somewhere deep down, a calm and dignified voice that was at once confident and accommodating. It was not his usual voice, but a voice that dangled the promise of success.

"Hello? International Bureau of Tourism Arts."

. . .

"What? What are you asking for?"

The calm, confident voice slithered away, like a python in a hole; gone was the readiness to negotiate and reach middle ground, and gone was the prospect of success. A rough, dry and sharp voice came from the roof of his mouth – the voice he used at home when he called the maid or when he argued with his mother to get her to lend him money or when he said good-bye to inaccessible women.

"No, sir, this is not the airport. This is the International Bureau of Tourism Arts."

Sana"s eyes were following a fly crawling on the wall when she suddenly became aware of affinities with that insentient thing. In that moment of seeing, she discovered some strange connection to the fly, and the thing swelled and shrank, raced along the wall and then dragged its feet. At one particular instant, Sana' thought the creature was gasping for air as it manoeuvred around a bump on the wall. Why won't it fly, she wondered. When Baha' turned off the air conditioner a moment later, the fly dropped out of view. Perhaps Sana' heard an odd shriek then, or even the sound of a sizeable corpus as it hit the surface of the turbid water. In that place, at that instant, a woman named Sana' coupled her life with that of a nameless fly.

"International Bureau of Tourism Arts. Yes, tourism arts. Open for a month now, so why has no one stepped out and benefitted from it?" Amin said. His vacuous stare sought some invisible creature to hold responsible for their predicament. "Not a single person. Somebody, somewhere had another destination in mind when he dialled us. Why?"

Somebody was knocking on the door and when Sana' opened it, a young man with dark eyes came in with a bagload of tools. He was here to fix the bathroom, he said. For the next few minutes the racket was nerve-wracking.

Baha' continued reading about Belgium in one of the flyers he had brought from Cook's, his mind brightened by a vision transparent as the wings of a butterfly. He saw the Swedish woman and could not really believe she was coming to fill his night with her pearly teeth. He looked at his watch.

Amin, eyes half closed, looked at the world map on the wall. A wide world full of colours he longed to wander through. Maps, airports and pharmacies rouse in him a mysterious yearning that at that moment reminded him of the creation of the Bureau of Tourism Arts. He had been reading about self-sufficiency in Henry David Thoreau's *Walden* when that mysterious yearning inexplicably seized his heart. Words on the page became glossy maps of open lands in brilliant colours. He heard the buzzing of numerous aeroplanes in a wilderness of tarmacs, landing and taking off. And he smelled, of course, perfumes, drugs and cosmetics in abundant pharmacies. In that flourishing, colourful, and sweet-smelling world, a full-fledged idea was born. Starting a tourism company.

He had just got his degree in Commerce, and words of advice about entrepreneurship still filled his ears. He ran to Baha's house. Though he and Baha' were worlds apart, they were classmates and partners in shameful pursuits or competitors in amorous adventures. Baha' was lukewarm at the beginning, then bit by bit details of the idea began to form images of costumes and languages and safaris and currencies, and even a vision of young women, beautiful and smiling, of curvaceous women, and of millions of blondes hungry for love. Baha' also saw a pristine and elegant office, a mecca in the midst of a sea of white, and he saw himself at the centre of it all.

"International Bureau of Tourism Arts," he said, slapping his forehead and then slamming the table with his fist. His head was still swarming with those visions and he believed he was challenging life itself, even destiny. Amin didn't hear what Baha' said, for his head, too, was touring as yet unheard-of places while the rattling table told him that the project had been approved.

Then he lost control of the idea. Baha' took over and insisted on doing things his own way, starting with spending the company's capital on the air conditioner, the bookcase, and the telephone. And Baha' insisted on writing the founding document in his own handwriting, and in that document he gave himself sixty per cent of the company's shares even though Sana' contributed two-thirds of the capital. He also put in the document something about "the responsibilities of management."

Sana' opened and closed her desk drawer, flipped through a bundle of papers in her hands, then rummaged through her handbag. The search stopped abruptly when she couldn't remember what she was looking for. Her hand on her cheek, she grumbled as she felt the silliness of her life. She felt she was acting out a role in a farce, and felt lost in a purposeless existence. If she died at that moment, she wouldn't have objected. That night when Baha' held her hand she liked it. Did she love him? Perhaps she did, but she cast a hopeless look in his direction.

The dark-eyed boy was done with the bathroom and he and his clattering bag were heading out. He didn't look at the three ghosts sitting in the office and didn't say good-bye; but just before he got to the door, he turned round terrified. Sana' had just leapt from her seat and shrieked as if touched by a demon. The entire International Bureau of Tourism Arts was shaking, sheets of paper scattered, and walls and windows shook in endless turmoil. The culprit, it turned out, was a cricket that had landed on Sana's head. It took her some time to get over her fright and embarrassment, and she sat there wrestling with a feeling of anxiety that had been expanding and shrinking all day and that had to find some outlet.

As if the landing of the cricket on her head was all she needed, it finally dawned on her and she got up as if possessed and grabbed her bag with determination. "What a joke – this company," she proclaimed. "Yes, a joke. I'm not coming back tomorrow." I'll go back to school and this time I'll be sure to succeed."

Slam!

The three ghosts were startled. A commotion outside dwarfed the mini–drama created by Sana"s declaration and they looked out of the window to find out what was happening down on the street. Sana's face twitched a little and her eyes narrowed, and she covered her face and sat in her chair shaking with uncontrollable laughter. Hoarse laughter that brought to mind the crowing of cocks, the crying of bereaved mothers, the braying of donkeys and the screams of a female in labour. Amin smiled and Baha' sat down in silence.

"What an ending," Amin said, his smile widening. "Down there on the street lies the body of the International Bureau of Tourism Arts. A vulgar name written in gilt letters on a crude sign. It's all down there." His disgust at the name found its ultimate expression.

Sana', still not quite over her fit of laughter, rose and left. Amin's hungry eyes followed her, and then he, too, followed. Baha' remained seated. He was not moved – no anger, concern or anxiety. In fact, the corners of his mouth displayed contentment. He was thinking of a Swedish beauty who would brighten his night with her pearly teeth. He looked at his watch.

"That is, if she comes," he said aloud to the decaying walls, the green telephone, the carpet that had seen better days, the air conditioner, and the mismatched books in their glass bookcase.

*Translated by Shakir Mustafa*

# The Furnace

## RACHIDA EL-CHARNI

The water bottle leered at the newly hired worker, urging her to quench her deep thirst. The controller who brought the bottle from the secretary's office had pulled it out of the folds of her dress and hidden it behind the boxes of fabric where she thought no one would see it but herself. The drops of sweat on the cold bottle tempted the worker to break her fast. She tried hard to think of something else by applying herself wholeheartedly to her work. However, her tired eyes continued to turn towards the bottle. Every time she raised her head the bottle was there like an impossible dream.

The boxes of fabric were piling up around her at a dizzying speed, adding to her anxiety and confusion. She was required to finish one thousand pieces. She had to clean each one individually, remove the numerous threads hanging from them, and cut off those that were too long. Then she had to place over each piece of fabric a cut-out of reinforced plastic that had a certain number of holes through which she marked the positions of the pockets on the blazers.

One of the Germans in charge of the factory had explained the work to her in a mixture of languages. She was delighted and surprised by the easy nature of the work, but soon discovered that she was required to keep her head buried in the fabric and work at the speed of a machine. She had to finish her load or be replaced.

The factory was constructed of large sheets of corrugated

iron that did not provide any protection from the heat of the sun. It had small, high windows. The atmosphere inside was suffocating because the temperature during that month had been over 40 degrees centigrade. The steam rising from the many irons being used added to the stifling atmosphere and increased the difficulty of working while fasting.

The supervisor, a stern look on her face, examined the girl's work from time to time to make sure that it had been done correctly. She would then leave and the new worker could hear the sounds of her high heels as she went along the lines, making recommendations to the other workers. She was single, in her forties, and looked miserable. She was a tiny woman and her small size contributed to her ugliness. The girl later learned that the others nicknamed her the Dwarf, Zakiyya the Dwarf.

There was a girl working on a huge iron nearby. She was sweating profusely, and the sweat had soaked her apron so that it clung to her ample body, revealing many of its intimate curves. She was probably chosen for the job because of her size. Her tired face revealed a certain innocence. She glanced furtively at the new worker as if she was looking for a reason to strike up a conversation with her. When the supervisor had walked away after one of her inspections, expressing her disapproval of the slow work by pursing her lips, the big girl tried to speak with the new worker.

"What's your name?" she whispered.

"Basma," came the reply.

"It is a beautiful name, it doesn't deserve to be mistreated," commented the girl with the iron.

Basma reflected, and said: "Our names cannot redeem us, and they cannot spare us the cruelty of fate."

"Listen Basma, do not spend too much time on each piece of fabric. Just remove the long threads that are visible and leave the short ones that need a lot of effort."

Basma replied, describing her difficulties with the job: "The scissors have worn me out and made my fingers bleed.

151

Don't you think a thousand pieces is a high number to demand of me?"

"Yes, it is, but you'll get used to it. Tell me, haven't you worked before?" the other girl inquired.

"No."

"What were you doing, then?"

"I was studying," replied Basma.

"What level did you reach?"

"Sixth grade in secondary," answered Basma.

The girl in charge of ironing was genuinely surprised. She stopped her work for a few seconds, and stared at Basma as though she was seeing her for the first time. Then she said: "You haven't found anywhere else to work except in a clothing factory?"

"I searched for a long time but was not successful," said Basma.

She had been looking for a job for some time. She had written many letters asking for work and one summer day she stuffed them all in her briefcase and distributed them to many ministries and companies. She waited for a reply for several months but received only one answer in which she was told there were no vacancies.

She wanted very much to find a job before her mother was forced to find work; she was even prepared to leave school and accept any work in order to spare her mother from working. She choked with silent tears at the mere thought of her mother, Mrs Khadija, daughter of Hajj 'Ali, going out to work as a cleaner in an office or hospital, clearing away rubbish, sweeping floors, and submitting to orders from all kinds of people."

Her father had been forced to retire the year before and during that time he had not been paid. At first he had been told his pay would be calculated according to a new financial system. Then he learned the computer had rejected his case because it was a very special one, and after that, they asked him for numerous documents and had sent him from one official to another. Finally, he exploded with rage, swearing at the computer, at the employees, and at the whole country. The police were called and took him to the station where he had to sign a statement which prohibited him from approaching those officials again.

He spent all the money he had saved and ended up working for a private company. Every evening he would return from work grim, morose, and suffering from terrible stomach pains. Having spent thirty-five years in a responsible position in one of the capital's government offices, it was difficult for him to find himself suddenly sitting behind a desk listening to the interminable babbling of colleagues interested only in showing off their most beautiful clothes. Moreover, he was working under the control of directors he was not allowed to question. His confrontations increased and his health deteriorated until he was forced to leave the work.

That morning Basma decided to go home only after she had found a job. She went to the industrial area and was given directions to the German-owned factory by a worker from Bata, the shoe firm.

When she got near and approached its big iron gates, she noticed a man unloading boxes from a huge truck. His honest demeanour encouraged her to speak to him. She called out to him and when he stopped unloading, she explained that she was looking for a job. He took a good look at her, then opened the factory gate and took her to the administration building. As she entered, she felt very excited but wished she could have been given time to collect herself together before meeting anyone.

A woman sitting at a desk behind a glass window raised her head when she heard the man's voice. She looked sleepy, and her dark-skinned face carried traces of heavy make-up. Her hair hung down her bare shoulders and no one could possibly guess its true colour because of the many rinses it had clearly endured. She looked down at the girl and asked her, yawning: "Do you have a sewing diploma?"

"No, but I reached sixth grade," answered the girl.

She shook her head and went on staring, surprised, then rubbed her eyes and looked in the other direction. The signs of sleepiness disappeared and then she said rather firmly: "Listen, we want girls who can sew, we do not need trainees."

Disappointment almost broke Basma's heart and she was on the verge of crying. As she started to drag herself sadly to the door, a tall man entered with an energetic step. She guessed from his features that he was the German in charge of the factory. He looked at her with a clever gaze that filled her heart with optimism. He asked in Arabic with a heavy German accent and stressing his Rs: "How old are you?"

" I'm seventeen," she replied.

He thought for a moment, scratched his forehead with his index finger, and then signalled to the secretary to register her. The secretary took out a large form and said to her: "You can work for us for thirty-five dinars a month. You're younger than the legal age of eighteen for working as a qualified person and so you can only be a trainee."

Without waiting for a reply, the secretary started filling in the application form. Basma thought to herself, "Thirty-five dinars! What misery! I'll be travelling from one end of the city to the other for thirty burning hot days only to receive this stupid sum." But she handed over her papers to the secretary, realising that at least it would be better than nothing.

She followed the German along a clean, narrow corridor with offices down both sides. The doors were open and revealed heavy wooden furniture and gloomy oil paintings. The atmosphere was rather dark, and austere German taste was visible everywhere.

The sound of the man's military-like steps grew quieter as they approached the machines. When he opened a large door Basma was overcome by a deafening hubbub mixed with the barely audible voice of the singer Warda. She saw a huge area filled with very modern sewing machines, operated by women whose faces showed extreme fatigue. They raised their heads, observing her furtively and then whispering among themselves. She felt she was the object of the whispering. Other women were singing along with Warda, repeating "In a day, in a night" as if to alleviate the burden of the work.

A bell rang and the workers dropped whatever they were doing and rushed in a strange frenzy to the rear of the sewing room. Dozens of them surrounded three taps. Their yelling and screaming increased as they pushed their way, as it happened, in her direction. Water flowed slowly, slowly from the taps, while the girls tried impatiently to wet their heads and chests. Later they left, wet and laughing, as though they had just experienced a rare pleasure. Basma drew back and stood near the door, feeling uneasy as she followed the strange sight and began to discover the secrets of the place. Some of the girls came to talk to her and she learned from them that the taps were turned off during work time to stop the women from going to the toilet and squandering water. She thought to herself, "What a mean way to save water."

She went with them to a large room where some women were lounging on a long wooden bench, while others were lying on the floor, each resting her head on the hip of the other. An argument broke out over the use of the bench and voices rose nervously. She expected it to lead to worse, but soon the confrontation turned into funny gestures that made everyone roar with laughter.

The bell rang again and the workers returned to their places, slow to start work. Yet as soon as the German supervisor appeared the pace picked up. Basma joined in the feverish activity, spending nerve-wracking hours trying to finish the thousand pieces that were required. She tried her best to prove she could do the job. When she had finished her work and the bell rang to go home, she felt better. The German came to check her work and despite his lack of comment, his attitude allayed her fears.

When he left, the big girl winked at her and said: "You

have to excuse him, he has learned only the language of work; as for the many Arabic terms for thanks, he is still unable to learn them."

The short, muscular man she had seen unloading the boxes stood near the doorway. He was examining the women's faces as they rushed to leave. They were making fun of him and flirting outrageously with him. When he saw Basma he called to her in a rough manner and motioned to her, with a nod of his head, to go to the nurse's room. She looked at the other workers, surprised, but they explained to her that she had to undergo a search, a procedure followed with each new worker. She overcame her anxiety and went inside.

The room was very small, and had a table, a bed and a few simple pieces of nursing equipment. A tall, broad-shouldered older woman approached her and asked to see her handbag. Basma emptied its contents on the table, revealing several papers, a book, some money, and a pair of small scissors. The nurse took the scissors and examined them as Basma explained that they belonged to her and that she had handed the others to the supervisor before she left. The nurse returned all the contents to the bag and Basma thought that she would be able to leave immediately, but to her great surprise the nurse ordered her to undress. Basma's face showed her deep anger and she felt like shouting at the nurse to vent her rage, but she calmed herself down and nervously began to undress. The nurse examined her clothes, searching the pockets carefully, and then returned them to her. Basma dressed quickly to hold back her tears.

She turned to the nurse and said: "I do not understand how you can accept to do this kind of police work."

A heavy silence filled the place, and as she finished buttoning her shirt Basma turned and saw the nurse looking very sad. She had retreated to a corner of the room and seemed to be in deep thought – as if Basma's remark had brought back pain she was doing her best to hide. As Basma was leaving, the nurse spoke: "I'm sorry, I'm only doing my job, my real profession is nursing. I graduated a few months ago and have not worked for a long time. I came here on the condition that I worked in my field but then they asked me to search the workers. I'm extremely embarrassed to be doing this but I have to because I couldn't find any other place to work."

As Basma left her new job, she was met by the sunlight, its rays shining in her tear-filled eyes. It was hot, but she felt that the weather was gentler than that of the furnace where she worked.

*Translated by Aida A Bamia*

# Black and White

## IDRISS EL-KHOURI

Exhausted, Sheherazade entered the lecture hall and took off the black scarf covering her head, letting her hair fall down freely all over – a film star preparing for a new role. Sheherazade peeled that navy blue coat off her generously proportioned back and sat down; this evening will be for work only, not for chatting with Africans; she put down her black leather bag on the grey table, then settled into the black chair. Oh, I'm dog tired, Sheherazade said, having at last sat down firmly, the way to the university restaurant has become quite a trip, and she pounced on her bag, bringing out some folded papers. Very well, I must transform what is in these papers with the typewriter. With that, Sheherazade got up, went to the other end of the hall and brought it: the German typewriter.

Now, there is no one with Sheherazade but God, and the grey tables and chairs, and the geographical maps hanging on the walls, and the telephone, and the blackboard spattered with chalk marks. There is no one with Sheherazade but herself and her desire to wait for Andopodo to enter the lecture hall. It is about two thirty, it is time for work, and soon her colleagues will be here and will sit in front of her or behind her, and Sheherazade will seem tiny in their midst, a mysterious question mark requiring an answer. Who is Sheherazade?.

The Arab who knows her well said: "She is from Warzazat,

south of the historic Red City." As for Professor Bernard, his daily lesson begins at about four and ends at five, only one hour, while she dies in banal discussions, awaiting appropriate words for reportage writing, isn't that so, Sheherazade?

Sheherazade answered that evening in the university restaurant: "Nevertheless, we have come here to study. In addition to the diploma, there are trips to the countries of Beethoven and Goethe."

The group sitting across the table from Sheherazade laughed, and she laughed too, chewing meat and bread. Andopodo was looking at Sheherazade sheepishly from under his white eyes as if she was a seductive piece of fat. Sheherazade is a good conversationalist, Andopodo told himself. And Sheherazade too said to herself: "Maybe I will call Hamadi when we leave the hall. I'd love to see Jean-Luc Godard's *Le Mèpris* with him."

Sheherazade is typing, tic toc tic toc tic toc tic toc tic toc tic toe, she stops to look over what she has typed, she has forgotten the word "production", tic toc tic toc tic toc, she stops – fuck, could have typed this article last week, but Binzirt was tempting, one must not waste opportunities: Hamadi, Samira and Mahfouz, all of them were wonderful during the trip, and now the assignment has entered the phase of execution, stop procrastinating! How could she have taken a trip to the desert(ed) south and not written a word on it? Sheherazade abides by one principle. Trips are for discovery. This is journalism. Sheherazade typed: "The X Island is famous for its numerous and beautiful hotels, and for its being the jewel of the south (Sheherazade remembered that on her return she had left Brigitte Bardot's second husband sunbathing with his second wife on the white sands), but X Island, despite all this, seems like a desert city; rather, a gateway to the desert. What is the importance of the sea here?

"That morning, we had been exploring it with the very excellent tourist bus: palm trees here and there, sand here and there, the sea here and there, misery, ah (between parentheses Sheherazade notes that this word is not beautiful), the wind was blowing from all directions, a little dust, then clouds of dust, and dead end. Where are the children? White sands and unpaved roads."

Sheherazade lifted her head: "Where are you, Aghadir, where are you Al-Husaima, where are you Al-Jadida?"

Sheherazade stopped typing momentarily to push away her hair, falling over her face, without rhyme or reason, from her right eye, at the end of the month she would be able to let David play freely with her hair. Sheherazade carried on typing: "We visited some farming co-operatives and some olive oil refineries that produce oil by primitive methods. It is great to import cows from Holland in order to increase the production of milk and butter. The presence of these factories, in the south, is a miracle, the dark young engineer told us, for in addition to the quantities of oil consumed locally, these refineries leap over the borders of neighbouring countries. We also visited modest houses whose occupants produce traditional artefacts."

Sheherazade said to Hamadi in the morning, clouds of dust flying around them: "Our traditional crafts are excellent. I suggest that you visit Marrakesh, Fes and Mèknes. For God's sake, try to . . ."

"Do you have co-operatives?"

"No."

"We have co-operatives, and because of that our products are shared."

Sheherazade was typing: "However, the situation for women seems to be backward."

The head of the Municipal Council told Sheherazade on the night of the 27th of Ramadan, before he went off for the tarawih prayer: "Listen, Miss, we are trying to raise the status of women among us. This is our objective, and they are beginning to read and learn crafts."

Sheherazade protested coyly: "Then why aren't there women in the streets?"

The head of the Municipal Council said, as he got ready to leave the hall for the mosque: "They are there when they find themselves obliged to go out – through necessity."

Al-Da'udi said at the door when they were leaving: "Sheherazade, there is no consumer civilisation here to make women want to go out, as in the capital."

Sheherazade laughed. Whatever. Those justifications did not convince her.

"She went on protesting," as Al-Da'udi told Muhsin, "on one premiss: her mini-skirt barely covering her thick thighs, Roger Vadim's interpretation of *Les Liaisons Dangereuses*, and her sitting in Maxim's in Paris."

Muhsin said to Al-Da'udi in the hotel, offering him a cigarette: "Her excuse is her repression in modern life."

Muhsin and Al-Da'udi laughed: this kind of conduct is what gives the bourgeois press a bad name. Prostitution, as some would call it.

Sheherazade stopped typing to contemplate the text: deformed and tired letters stared at her swollen eyes. What does this word mean? She bent over the sheet: "The Municipal Council of X City accepts many proposals to build tourist hotels along the entire shoreline, and each cubic metre is worth ten dirhams. Such capitulations benefit the growing tourism, as the head of the Municipal Council said."

Sheherazade stopped writing. There are noises, then the sound of quick trots up the steps outside. Claude hurled himself through the door like a ball. Claude said, "Bonjour", Samuel said, "Bonjour", Samba said, "Bonjour", and Andopodo said, "Bonjour".

These are the black, Cameroonian faces, faces that laugh all the time without showing any signs of fatigue, but Sheherazade cannot stand them – except one, the face of Andopodo, handsome, humorous, humane, serious, and father of three children who are now eating coarse bananas and running towards the rivers. Andopodo is the shore where Sheherazade longs to throw herself and disappear for a while, eating bananas and cocoa, wearing traditional dresses, swimming in the rivers, running in the jungles, and taking photos of herself that she will keep in an album. Something will happen this evening.

When the Cameroonian line breaks another line appears: mixed, adolescent, shaky, a line that lives every day without a cause, and they say together in an uneven, unruly voice, "Bonjour", then scatter around the hall like football players on the field. Hamadi and Hussein sat at the back, Bouchu'aib and Abdullah in front, and Samira, Aziza and Mahfuz in the middle. These are familiar faces by now, young faces, though with too much make-up. Is a response required? Sheherazade replied coldly: "Bonjour." She called Andopodo, who was leafing through the newspapers.

Andopodo: "How are you?"

Sheherazade: "All right, but I feel tired."

Andopodo: "I can see that on your face."

Sheherazade: "I didn't sleep well last night, as usual. I went to the cinema."

Andopodo: "Oh, very good. What did you see?"

Sheherazade: "The film *Mon Amour, Mon Amour.*"

Andopodo: "It sounds like *Hiroshima, Mon Amour.*

Sheherazade: "Yes."

Andopodo: "And how was the party?"

Sheherazade: "Fabulous. I was with Samira and Hamadi."

Andopodo: "Too bad. I, on the other hand, went back to the hotel early to find a letter waiting for me. My son is ill."

Sheherazade: "Kamka?"

Andopodo: "Yes, Kamka, he is down with sleeping sickness, which is plaguing our country these days."

Sheherazade: "I read about that in the papers."

Andopodo: "From typhoid to sleeping sickness, what luck!"

They laughed and laughed, while others were chattering at the back or, at the front, reading newspapers. Andopodo looked from Scheherazade's full, spotty face, to her bare thighs. So much meat, but for what? Desire was coursing through Andopodo, ready to jump out of his mouth, but how? Last time, when they were sitting side by side in the cinema, Andopodo could not control himself when Schcherazade crossed her legs, putting her right thigh over her left, each was a burning fire. Andopodo remembered his wife. She was not as seductive as Sheherazade, but she had her very own magic. What is attractive about Sheherazade? As long as there is a burning body, the fire must be put out. Andopodo thought of inviting her to his room, but he remembered his dark skin. Sheherazade said to Hamadi last Saturday evening: "I really like talking to Andopodo."

"How come?"

"Because he is the only one who strikes my fancy, as simple as that. He is a serious young man."

"I'm scared for you, Sheherazade, I swear to God."

"Why?"

"Rape?"

"What I care about is my reputation, not my honour. With Andopodo, there will be no rumours."

"You're a traitor."

"I despise you. I was an idiot in the beginning."

"You're acting."

They parted in the evening at the bus station.


Andopodo said: "You're very bright."

Sheherazade said: "Why do you say these things?"

"Because you deserve to hear them."

"I used to hear these things from Monsieur Jacques."

"Really?"

"Monsieur Jacques was a close friend of André Gide. Do you know André Gide?"

"Of course I know him. In high school I read his *Pastoral Symphony* and then *The Counterfeiters* and *The Fruits of the Earth*. He is a great writer."

"He used to come to Tunis."

"He went there to find a cure for his sexual sickness."

They laughed and laughed.

And the others were chatting, "the Viet Cong are surrounding the Khe Sangh Base."

"General Westmoreland is absolutely incapable of completing his mission successfully."

"Johnson is uncomfortable with the idea of attacking the Viet Cong."

"Eshkol-Johnson talks."

"Tonight is the opening night for Irma La Douce".

"Growing closeness between Bonn and Belgrade, and Moscow is worried."

"Tito in Aswan."

"Israel wants Jarring to be an intermediary between Israel and the Arab states."

Andopodo too was looking through the papers. Sheherazade wants him even if he is black. It would be wonderful if this could happen. But he thinks she wants him because it is fashionable.

Andopodo said: "Shall we continue our conversation this evening?"

"Yes."

"You know we're going out together?"

"Yes."

"Have you written your article?"

"I haven't finished it yet."

"You must finish it."

Sheherazade smiled seductively and exchanged long looks with Andopodo. Professor Bernard came in and sat down in front of everyone. This is the daily lesson. Sheherazade leaves her hand in Andopodo's.

*Translated by Wen-chin Ouyang*

# The Sweetest Tea with the most Beautiful Woman

## TAREK ELTAYEB

Listening to the radio is prohibited
Smoking is prohibited
Drinking tea is prohibited
Laughter and jokes are prohibited
Sleep is prohibited
Sitting down is prohibited
Even dreams are prohibited

The list of prohibited things is long and embraces everything new. We know nothing of permissions. Before making any movement or action we must ask which list it comes under. Things that are permitted can shift to the list of prohibitions on a whim, and they don't go back the other way. This is what life has become – rigid, fixed and as interminable as the list of prohibitions. And the place has become restricting and depressing in this wide, empty tract of land.

I take up my weapon now and take my turn on guard. The final shift. My hasty companion wakes me, snatches my dream and goes to sleep with it. He leaves me with my eyes open in shock. Every awakening here is to shock, we don't wake up to anything else. I sigh to relieve some of the anxiety that is spreading in my chest and it stops at my throat. I get up, take my weapon and go to my place of duty where the snoring reverberates in my ears like the mockery of devils.

I am trying to recall my dream. It was a fabulous dream. I don't know exactly what it was. Before the moment of shock I was in another world utterly at odds with this roughness and coarseness. There was some woman in my usurped dream. I cannot remember her features. That idiot, if he'd left me a moment longer I'd have been able to get hold of her by now. She was repeating my name in such a soft voice, when the loathsome sound of "Hey you, soldier boy! . . . Private! Get up! . . . Goddamn this place!"merged with her voice. It'll be nine weeks and two days today. I see nothing of the world but this god-forsaken army camp and these scowling faces. The voices are vile, the looks are crazed, the language foul, the food repulsive, the drinks worse and sleep is disturbed. Nothing but orders. Orders or punishments. And our compliance always expressed in polite, prepared utterances; memorised and hypocritical. Nine weeks two days and I, with five others, have been sentenced to an indefinite revocation of my holiday for some unwarranted offence.

The officer is happy with these offences. He sees his importance in terms of the harsh penalties he meets out. To humiliate others gives him a sense of a certain prominence in the hierarchy of coercion and humiliation issuing from on high. He gives vent to the dejection of his spirit on our bodies and our souls, for there are none lower in the pecking order than us. Sometimes we look for the weak among us to pour what we can of the venom of our humiliation against them. Together we all eat, and together we laugh. Each one of us curses another at the slightest excuse. We take sides, we break allegiances, we steal things from one another, we plot against each other. And the humiliation remains part of us.

Nine weeks, five days and everything repeats itself with a deathly boredom. It is August and we are in the desert; in a military camp in the desert. The sun and the officers ravage us by day and the night shifts and insects complete the matter at night. Nothing of our humanity is left but past memories. We combine what we can recall of these with a little patience and song, and sham laughter – prohibited of course. Here, I hear daily of the failures of every soldier and the struggles of every officer. Occasionally I am rooted to the spot by someone weaving fantasies as one of us begins to tell a story with the scent of woman in it – even if he has embroidered it with lies and stuffed it with exaggeration. At our evening gatherings we listen closely to the story-teller. We wander off with his stories, wandering ever more freely if it is a story about a loved one. On such nights each one of us is Sheherazade's sacrifice, and in the mornings, with our orders, every one of us is a sacrifice to the homeland.

In this detention I have almost forgotten the voice and scent of a woman. I live off the false stories that I hear and the recollection of remnants of dreams stolen from me. I transform the stolen dreams into my daydreams and complete the delusion of my days.

What could be more miserable than this, this separation from women! What are we supposed to do, kept away from them like this! Are we preparing ourselves for war, just to be able to win for ourselves as many as possible? It is laughable. Give me my self, alone, with just one; that would be enough. I'll leave this war and weapons and destruction and killing, just for the winning of the greatest number of women possible, to you lot. Madness draws nearer and an admission of numbness rises from tortured humanity. I have nothing left of my humanity but the weakened threads of feeling. I have become like the lamb limping before the wolf. There is no running any more. Just an attempt to satisfy the grovelling bleats and lecherous howls.

"Wake up, soldier!"

The officer raps it out in a voice that makes the whole camp quake. I am next to him, about five paces away. The words pierce me and kill all that is left.

Nine weeks five days. The day has got stuck and it doesn't want to pass. It is now five pm. I go into the officer's room to submit three letters that have arrived for the soldiers. He must open them himself and read them before they can reach the boys. Maybe he'll find in them plans for a plot against state security, and thus his promotion. I see a three-day permit without a name on it, signed, on his desk. Without much deliberation I shove it into my tunic pocket and leave.

I leave the camp at a run, having first checked up on the movement of traffic coming in and going out and the whereabouts of the officer and guards. I run for three miles and then stop a lorry coming out of one of the camps. I don't know where it will head, but I jump up into it. I want to disappear and let it go wherever it wants even if it is going back to the camp.

I'm in the back for about half an hour. The lorry driver stops and knocks on the inner window at me, asking if I'm getting down here or whether he should take me with him into the western camp. I hear him mention the word 'camp' and jump down without replying, thanking him in his wing mirror with a wave of my hand.

I see a tree and houses in the distance. I hear the chirping of birds, and dogs barking, and then the indistinct voices of people. I hasten cautiously in the direction of the voices. I finger the permit so that no antagonist from the military police can hinder my way and I am reassured by its presence. I run faster and then stop, suddenly, next to a school from which rises the clamour of school kids. I feel drunk on the voices of the childhood I have lost, and even more drunk when I see her.

The most beautiful of all the things I see in this place; no, the most beautiful thing I have ever laid eyes on in this world. There she is, sitting, making tea. And no one is there but an old man, a few metres away from her, who looks into nothing and sips from his cup with great slurps, enjoying the taste, day dreams and fantasies. I ask for a cup of tea.

"Pleasure, my love."

Thus she replies in a voice that makes me tremble; a more beautiful voice than this I have never heard and never shall. For she is the woman for whose sake, and with whom, we stayed up all those nights. She is the Sheherazade of the stories, the smile of the sad ones. I look at her before me. Nine weeks and five days. I do not move my eyes from her face. She looks at me and smiles. The smile is for me alone. I want to hear her voice once more, so I say: "I'd like four spoons of sugar."

"Pleasure, my love!"

She repeats what she'd said in an even sweeter tone, as though saying something new. I am addicted to her voice. I search for another question that I may hear that tone again. I find nothing. I go mute and leave the listening to my eyes. I contemplate the veins of her life, long and prominent, on the back of her hand. She wants to cover her head, and a few wisps of hair fall out from under her Bedouin-worked scarf onto her forehead, enhancing her grace. She puts her hand out to me with a glass of hot tea. Intentionally, I touch the hand. I grasp the glass with both hands. At that moment I recall the dream that the loathsome soldier stole from me.

I savour the sweetest tea I have ever drunk in my life, I smile at her with a smile that speaks louder than words, and I awaken to the tones of her voice, honeyed with that tremor of the voices of kind grandmothers, saying: "Here you are, son! Is there enough sugar?"

*Translated by Rebecca Porteous*

# The Picture

## HASSAN NASR

In our home, we have a picture hanging in the middle of one wall of the sitting-room. Nobody knows who first hung it there. Our home is a large house that my father inherited from his forefathers. The picture is old, and our home has a lot of old furniture such as chairs with high, decorated backs, a big green box inlaid with white and red shells, which my grandmother has kept and in which she puts her things, a wooden wardrobe which woodworm has bored through and which is cracked and splintered and which no member of the family pays attention to any longer; nor does any of them pay attention to those worm-eaten chairs. However, the picture has always preserved its newness.

From its high place on the wall, it looks down on us, attracts our attention, and strengthens our love for this home and our attachment to it. By being in the sitting-room, it has always drawn everyone's gaze. Its importance is heightened by the fact that it sits alone on the "throne" of the wall. Its wide gilt frame has kept its lustre as well as its solidity and has resisted the attacks of the woodworm that has bored into the other pieces of furniture. The wall of the room is big and empty. The picture does not fill the emptiness, neither by its size nor by its being there. Yet its being there is sufficient to fill the whole world, all by itself. The picture does not represent anything. Yet it represents everything. It represents the surface of the sea and nothing but the sea, stretching out like freedom – wide and blue. Looking at it comforts your soul, brings quietness into you, and gives rest to your nerves.

Every member of the family has his own room for himself and his dependents. But we all – brothers and cousins – share the sitting-room. It is the only room which unites us and we all go to it and are attached to it and its furniture and especially the picture which, in our eyes, fills the whole world.

This evening, I am alone in the sitting-room, crossing it back and forth, listening to my wife's screams coming from the next room– she is in labour and I eagerly wait for the first person to bring me news. My waiting goes on and on and I can hardly settle in one place. Then, several moments pass in which I no longer hear any moaning. The pain has stopped and I imagine I hear the cry of the new baby. I breathe deeply and throw myself on the nearest chair to rest.

No sooner do I regain my breath than I hear something large falling to the floor. I jump to my feet as I see with consternation that the old picture has crashed down. As I rise, a glass of water tips over and water spills on to the floor. Shards of crystal and glass are mixed up and land in all directions, while the water runs over the colours as though the sea has overflowed from inside the picture.

I look at the wall and it seems like a bald head, without beauty. At this moment, my brother comes in, followed by my aunt and niece, to convey the news to me. My wife has given birth to a beautiful baby boy. They look at me. As for me, I point to the picture and say: "Did you hear the thump as it fell? Look! The picture is in pieces."

My brother takes me by the hand, saying: "Don't be distressed. Come, we'll replace it with the picture of the new baby."

When I hear the baby crying, I forget everything. I no longer remember whether there ever was a picture that has actually ended up in pieces.

*Translated by Issa J Boullata*

# Sa'diya Fell from the Balcony

## SABRI MOUSSA

On Friday morning Sitt I'tidal woke up early. The moment she opened her eyes she screamed in bed: "Sa'diya . . . bitt ya Sa'diya! Come and find my slippers!"

Sa'diya entered the bedroom, rubbing her red eyes. She bent her thin peasant body under the bed looking for the slippers. She placed them on the feet of her mistress, then stood back waiting for orders.

"Bitt, what are you standing there for? Get moving and get the flat tidied up by the time I get out of the bathroom."

Sa'diya quickly left the room. Sitt I'tidal got off the bed, scratching her fat white body. An hour later when she came out of the bathroom, Sa'diya was in the living room. She was standing on a dining-room chair so that she could reach the glass surface of the sideboard. Sitt I'tidal screamed: "Get down, girl! Your foot could slip and then you'd fall on the glass breaking everything on it! Run off and get Ahmad the concierge!"

Sa'diya slipped through the front door of the flat, jumping lightly down the stairs from the third floor to call on Ahmad while her mistress went into the bedroom and sat in front of the mirror.

Today was Friday and the husband of Sitt I'tidal was on a business trip to Tanta. She had promised her three children Muna, Azmi and Ala' that she would take them to visit their grandmother in Shubra. She sat thinking about that tedious visit while she was putting on her make-up. She dreaded the outing to her mother-in-law that day . . . the old woman adored her grandchildren and would inevitably insist that they stay for lunch. Sitt I'tidal would then be forced to listen to all her problems. She would have preferred to postpone the visit till the late afternoon. But then she had made arrangements with her friend Umayma.

Sitt I'tidal was pursing her lips as she put on lipstick when an idea jumped into her head. Her cold eyes widened. She could find an excuse to leave the grandmother's house before noon: she had left the girl Sa'diya alone in the flat. "Impossible, Tante! The girl is alone and I locked her up in the flat. Maybe she would fall from the balcony or do some injury to herself."

Sitt I'tidal's face brightened with the solution. The maid brought in the heavily built conceirge who was sent off to buy breakfast. "Shall I go ahead and wake up Miss Muna and Master Azmi?""No, let them sleep until breakfast is ready."

By ten o'clock Sitt I'tidal was dressed up to the nines and Sa'diya had finished putting the shoes on the feet of the three children. She stood watching Muna in her colourful dress.

"Bitt ya Sa'diya . . . we're not going to be late . . . do you understand? You eat now, then wash the dishes and clean up the bathroom after the children. I want you to sit in the living-room, and don't move until I get back!"

She took the children and closed the front door. Sa'diya stood behind it listening to the key turning. Her stressed face relaxed and its childish features resurfaced. At the sound of the children's feet moving away, she started running in the hallway singing to herself and sat down at the table unselfconsciously eating the leftovers.

Sa'diya is always happy when her mistress leaves her alone in the flat. In moments like these she feels free to do what she wants without being watched. When she had finished eating she carried the plates to the kitchen. She washed them, and then cleaned the bathroom. She went into the children's bedroom and pulled out Muna's doll, Azmi's car and the colouring book of Ala'. She pushed the car round in a circle and then held the doll tightly to her as she turned the pages of the colouring book. The doll was unresponsive and Sa'diya soon got bored with its unvaried sounds. She put the toys back in the bedroom and went out onto the balcony.

The balcony faced the main street. Sa'diya saw a group of children running after a man banging a drum. There was a second man wearing a clown's conical hat and a girl carrying a sack. They all turned onto a side street. The children were screaming gleefully and clapping.

Sa'diya gripped the railing of the balcony as she swung her body to the right to see what was going on. She saw the children form a circle with the two men and the girl in the centre ready to demonstrate their tricks. Fire was coming out of the tall man's mouth, the one wearing the hat. The drumming was repetitive and the children began clapping to the beat. Sa'diya wished she were sitting down there with them. She felt her waist almost split as she leaned over further to see more clearly what was going on. She was mesmerised, her fingers going numb on the metal railing and her toes gradually lifting off the ground so that she would not miss one detail.

The excuse of Sitt I'tidal did not work. The grandmother insisted that the children stay for lunch. Sitt I'tidal was forced to join them. She left them at three to return to the flat. The moment the porter saw her he said: "Where have you been, ya Sitt I'tidal? The girl Sa'diya fell from the balcony and the ambulance took her to al-Qasr al-Ayni hospital. You have to go there."

What news! She beat her hand against her chest!

In al-Qasr al-Ayni hospital they told her the girl had died and that she was required to go to the police station for the inquiry. She took a taxi and stopped at her friend Umayma's. She waited until her friend got dressed and took her along.

At the police station she told them that the girl had been

working for her for two years and that she was an afreet, a lit-tle devil — all she did was hang over the balcony all day long watching who was coming and going — and that she was totally useless around the house. The officer thanked her with a smile and temporarily closed the case.

At around six o'clock the Mercedes taxi stopped in front of the main post office on Adli Street. Sitt I'tidal pulled down her tight skirt and bent over her friend as she was getting out. "This won't take a moment Umayma, OK?"

She entered the telegraph office and pulled a sheet of paper and sent a telegram to Sheikh Mohammad Abu Awad in Kafr Ghannam. "Sa'diya fell from the balcony. Come urgently to pick her up."

Then she went out to the taxi and told the driver: "Cinema Cairo, ya usta." She then turned to her friend and said: "This one is on me."

Umayma looked at the fat body of her friend and her cold eyes as if she was seeing her for the first time. Sitt I'tidal said to her: "What? What's the matter? Why are you looking at me like that?"

Umayma said: "Nothing . . . I am just surprised that you would want to go to the cinema, considering the circum-stances."

Sitt I'tidal waved her arm in annoyance: "Don't make such a fuss! One's nerves have been shot through all day."

*Translated by Mona Zaki*

# Rasmiya! Your Turn is Next!

## SABRI MOUSSA

The early days of September. The Nile across from Jazirat Badran Street in Rawd al-Farag. The red waters are still; some children are playing by the river and the time is sunset. One child suddenly points to the water: "Boys! What's that over there?" The other children look to where he is pointing, to see the water toying with a jute sack close to the shore. They exclaim in excitement: "There must be fish in it! Let's open it!" They drag the sack out. The boys scream and flee in terror. The sack contained the remains of a human body: two legs, two arms and a woman's breast.

❧

The first week of September. The police continue to investigate the unknown identity of the murdered woman.

❧

The second week of September. The search leads to the governorate of Giza after the Homicide Unit concludes that the body floating in the sack had come from the south. The head of the murdered woman is still not found and her identity remains unknown. The police continue searching for women who have disappeared under mysterious circumstances.

Mid-September: an old quarter close to the Corniche in Rawd al-Farag known as Hikr Abu Duma. Most of its residents are from Tama in the Upper Egyptian governorate of Suhag. They work in water transportation between Cairo and Upper Egypt. The time is night and the still boats lie in the dark waters of the quay facing the quarter.

A small lantern hangs in a docked boat that has not yet emptied its cargo. In the hull, some men gather around the weak light smoking their pipes, drinking tea and talking about the dismembered body – the one found in the jute sack.

"Boys, don't you think it could be Rasmiya?" says one of them suddenly.

They put down their tea glasses and look at one another in astonishment. "Rasmiya!"

"Yes, Rasmiya . . . the divorced wife of Abd al-Qawi . . . the daughter of al-Hajj Baraka, the head of the workers."

"But Rasmiya is in prison, boys!"

"Where have you been? You're not in this world! She was imprisoned for three months and then she got out and is staying at her father's. But the girl is, as you all know. . . she can't keep away from men . . . and al-Hajj Baraka swore in front of the entire quarter of Abu Duma that he had to kill her."

"It is not at all far-fetched that the man would have done it! He has a hard heart . . . like iron."

"Just stop it now . . . Let's not talk about this. One of you blow out the lamp now."

"Are we going to keep quiet about this?"

"Then, what do suggest we do, Ibn Zakiya? A woman wants to go the wrong way . . . and her father kills her . . . Why should you interfere with him, eh?"

Ibn Zakiya remains silent, saying nothing. Then Muhammadayn asks: "Where is Abd al-Qawi now?"

"He landed before sunset."

"Watch out no one says a word of this to him . . . do you all understand? You must all keep your mouths shut."

Abd al-Qawi returns to his boat that night after all the men had turned in. He circles al-Hajj Baraka's house hoping to catch a glimpse of Rasmiya. He fails. He tries to find out some of her news and learns that she disappeared weeks ago. The image of the dismembered body in a jute sack disturbs him: Al-Hajj Baraka must have fulfilled his oath and wiped out the shame; he had given a man's word in front of them all of what he would do and here he is . . . he has actually done it.

Abd al-Qawi sinks into a whirlpool of conflicting emotions. He remembers that ill-fated night. He was away on a trip that lasted a month and a half – his work always divided between Cairo and Upper Egypt. The yearning for his wife during these trips killed him. The journeys made him long for Rasmiya and as soon as the boat docked in Rawd al-Farag he would jump out and rush home. He would surprise her. As it turned out, the surprise lay in store for him. He found Rasmiya in bed with a stranger. That night he went mad. He screamed. He swore to divorce her. Rasmiya was imprisoned for three months on account of adultery.

But, at this moment Abd al-Qawi feels a strong yearning for her – now that she has become a dismembered body in a sack. He wishes he could touch her with his hand and tell her a word or two. Suddenly, his heart fills with resentment toward al-Hajj Baraka, the hard man who allowed himself to become a law above the law. He decides to notify the police.

ↈ

The third week of September. The police in Rawd al-Farag station are investigating the report presented by Abd al-Qawi and they surprise al-Hajj Baraka with a visit. The broad-shouldered man welcomes them with a sarcastic smile and says carelessly: "You must be here asking about the sack that you found in the Nile."

"No, we have come to ask about Rasmiya."

"Rasmiya escaped weeks ago . . . but where would she hide? Sooner or later, she will be found and I will fulfil the oath . . . Why don't you sit down and have some tea?"

The police leave al-Hajj Baraka certain that the mystery is close to getting solved. The identity of the murdered woman has ceased to be anonymous. She must be Rasmiya and this man her killer. But where is the evidence? The police continue their search.

The police go to the court of Rawd al-Farag and obtain the case file of Rasmiya. They send the finger-prints to the expert so a match could be made with those of the unidentified woman. If these prints matched . . . that would be the best evidence.

&

The last days of September. The expert sends in his report. The finger-prints do not match.

The mystery returns to darkness. The identity of the nameless murdered woman remains unknown. It was simply a matter of a different set of prints.

Rasmiya! Your turn is next!

*Translated by Mona Zaki*

# Butrus: A Distant Hazy Face

## MANSOURA EZELDIN

While my grandfather looked after his personal affairs, I would turn to another who went by the name of Butrus, and whom I had pictured as a dark youth with smooth long dark hair and sharp eyes. Butrus was the son of the priest of the Church of Our Lady Rebecca, or 'Saint Rrrebecca' as Edith haughtily insisted on calling her.

He was seventeen years old when, on 22 March 1976, he came to visit my uncle. They both went off to the banks of the Nile. My uncle returned a short time later, petrified, while the other settled into the coldness of the riverbed. That evening, I came into the world.

My grandfather would gather us around him and start telling us the story of my uncle's friend who was enticed away by the fairies and how his parents went off to the Nile in search of him while people gathered on the river bank to help or watch. By midnight, they had still not found him, so they walked away with their lanterns, and throughout the following week kept returning to try to find him. But the boy had dissolved in the water "like a grain of salt", as my grandfather said.

The boy's father went back to where he had come from. Meanwhile Butrus remained like a corner-stone in the history of our family. His story could be relied upon to frighten the children whenever the need arose, with the occasional embellishment. And so, one would talk about his bicycle, which he had dragged along on his last visit to a school friend. On another occasion, his glasses and the chemistry book he was holding would be the main features of the story. I was the only one to enquire what Butrus looked like. Grandfather answered impatiently: "He was tall and well-built, and had blue eyes like the English."

But I insisted that he was pleasantly dark with sharp features and bright eyes. My grandfather replied sarcastically: "And how would you know, Miss Know-it-all?"

Angry, I shut up.

When I recall my grandfather now, I see a wicked person who used to tease me about not having a role in his tales and who wanted to monopolize the power of story-telling that granted him extreme, though temporary, importance.

Butrus's ghost was the loyal companion of our childhood evenings. It was enough for a mother to utter his name for the children to start crying from fear.

A year after he drowned, his ghost started to wander in the fields surrounding the river. Grandfather insisted that the ghost appeared every time he lingered by his banana trees. It was Butrus "himself" reading his chemistry book. And when Grandfather approached him, Butrus would say: "Why are you so late, Uncle? You must go, lest you be harmed. How is your son Mohammad? Please give him my best and tell him Butrus would like to see him."

Having completely captured our attention with his words, Grandfather would then add that he had obtained a binding promise from Butrus not to harm any member of our family.

I used to tell my friends about Butrus, embroidering the stories in my own way. I would say, for example, that he had appeared to me and given me Solomon's ring which I was keeping in a secret place and using to realise all my dreams, or that he had told me I was the most beautiful girl he had ever seen. They would yield to my stories with some fear and much bewilderment.

At high school, I met beautiful Edith who had jet-black hair and eyes that left one's heart in pain. I once asked her about the priest of Lady Rebecca Church whose son Butrus had drowned. Her black eyes glistened and she replied with a kind of aristocratic hauteur: "You mean 'St Rrrebecca'? I don't know, maybe, but that was ages ago."

Edith never paused over such details. She moved on to another subject and never even asked about Butrus.

Her French was fluent, and her eyes knew how to conquer eyes that faced them, before withdrawing their gaze, leaving only the pain of incomprehension. Edith, who pronounced the letter 'r' the French way, and who came to our town because of the work of her engineer father, mocked everything around her. Her laughter was defiant and she made gratuitous humorous comments about those around her, like a gambler who faces the loss of all his possessions with an indifferent smile. But I once surprised her crying as she spoke about the Virgin Mary. She was mumbling with a deference that was at variance with her usual abandon, an abandon that knew how to tempt hearts and win their compassion by displaying with calculated precision a kind of weakness.

Edith had been envious of the Virgin Mary. When she told the priest, he stroked her hair with his hand and uttered words that she forgot as time went by although she could still feel the shudder they sent through her as she uttered with him and the others: "Blessed art thou amongst women and blessed is the fruit of thy womb."

I knew from the beginning that there was some mysterious link between us that had brought us together. My question about Butrus was the way I reached her, and her tales about Mary and St George, whose pictures I saw on the walls of her room and in her wallet, and about Salome and Esther, the proffered Host for our friendship.

Beginnings have the lure of discovery and endings a bitter

taste. This must be what Butrus realised as he settled, to his surprise, in the depths, and what Edith came to realise as she was bidding me farewell, shedding tears that she described in her first letter to me as "vulgar", saying that the whole scene was vulgar in spite of ourselves. As for me, I felt the pain of endings when I went to her later to win her back.

Whenever Grandfather was not invoking the name of Butrus, I would be telling her long tales in her room, which was full of the pictures of saints while she would be opening my mind to names like Flaubert, Hugo and Rousseau and reading French poetry to me which she then translated. She seemed even more attractive when she smiled triumphantly at her feeling of superiority, a feeling that nevertheless incensed me. But she seemed small and uncomfortable before the admiring looks that her darling "Peter"gave me. Peter, whom I used to call Butrus, welcomed this name with serene laughter, saying: "What's the difference? I'm going to call you 'Marianne', how about that?"

Peter left Edith alone but that was nothing to do with me, for all that linked me to him was the resemblance between him and the picture I had drawn in my imagination of a boy who lived in the distant past and who drowned on the day I was born.

One distant day, she sat next to me in her room, which suddenly seemed very narrow, and told me that I was closer to her than the Virgin Mary and all the pictures she kept, and bade me farewell with tears that she later described as vulgar.

But there seemed to be malice in her gift to me of a photograph of her and Peter, claiming that she had no photographs of her alone, adding: "And this way I can also get rid of the last picture of myself with Butrus. Isn't this how you like to call him?"

A while later, I paid her a visit. She was there before me with her amazing presence, her light darkness, her captivating look and a feeble sadness in her eyes, a noble sadness that reminded me of the pictures of women saints that hung in her room. But she was far beyond my reach, despite our desperate efforts to keep hold of that which bound us together.

As I was leaving her, there was a distant, hazy face looming before me of a boy who went by the name of Butrus, a face moving away from me of a friend named Edith, and the mocking laughter of my grandfather.

*Translated by Nada Elzeer*

# The Flower Seller

## Mohammed Zefzaf

The maid killed her. The flower seller was old so she could not defend herself. Before she killed her, the maid locked the door and took everything she could. Then she tried to get away by climbing out through another window on the third floor. She slipped and killed herself. She lay on the pavement, her loot beside her. So, the flower seller died and the maid too. One in her flat and the other on the pavement. People collected round the body on the pavement, some looked up to the flat and no one knew if anyone had managed, in turn, to steal what they could.

The firemen, the police and the ambulance arrived, of course. They took the body that was in the flat and the one on the street. Both were taken away in the same vehicle to where they perform autopsies even though there was no need for one in this case. The main thing is that the two bodies were taken away. People stayed around; maybe they did not have anything to do. One man said: "The flower seller was Senegalese. She grew up in a convent. That is why she only spoke French." Another said: "No. She spoke Arabic even though she was black. She was not Senegalese. Her mother was Moroccan from Ouarzazate. For some reason, her mother left her with the nuns. It is true that she was older than me but that's what they used to say. Her mother worked in the homes of foreigners. No one knows who got her pregnant." Someone added: "The blacks are everywhere; they work in construction and as gardeners in villas. One of them must have got her pregnant."

The truth is no one knew anything about the flower seller. She kept to herself. She was well dressed, walked her dog on Sundays and talked to him. She had a shop facing a church that had been abandoned by its faithful, except for a monk who lived in one part of it. He knew the Qur'an by heart and practised shameful things with some of the young Moroccans in return for helping them get visas and work permits to France.

The black flower seller lived above her shop, on the third floor. She would look out of her window at the empty church. Sometimes a cross would dangle from a gold chain which she would try to hide because she was afraid it might get stolen or that people would say she was Christian. No one knew whether she was Christian or Muslim because she did not speak about these things. The main thing was she was black. That was enough. And she had a dog she would take on walks and she'd give alms to beggars even though they hadn't asked her. It seems she knew what charity was about – the same charity with which her mother handed her over to the nuns; the same charity with which the monk gave out passports and other things. The door of the church was wide open which explained its outpouring of charity. The door of the flower seller was also open but it was narrow. It wasn't exactly open to everyone; mostly to old foreign women – Spanish, Italian, French and some Moroccans who had married Europeans. Women whose husbands had died and were left behind in the quarter. They visited and gossiped about one another. They mostly gossiped about their maids, changing them the same way they changed their underclothes out of fear of some imaginary diseases, all part of old age. The maids stole carefully, except for that demented one who had the audacity to kill.

So, the maid killed the flower seller. She probably robbed her several times before actually killing her. The black flower seller died; the maid died; and before them an old Spaniard who bought flowers from her once a week died. He was around seventy and never married. He drank all day and would pass regularly by the flower shop and talk to her for about half an hour. He never told her if he had actually married. The flower seller would speak about the deceased Spaniard and no one knew whether he was her friend, husband, brother or some other relative. The main thing was that the deceased was mentioned when women would talk to one another about men. It seems that he was well-dressed and decent. He had some position in the government during the French occupation. It was also hinted that he favoured some kind of light drink, that he loved dogs, and playing boule, especially in the evenings and at weekends. The flower seller didn't change her maids the way her old women friends did. At times she would pretend to forget to pay them. The maids left of their own accord: some got married and divorced soon after and some completely disappeared. And the doors of prison were open to all. Also the mental hospitals, if you can call them that. Speaking of hospitals, no one knows if they took the bodies of the flower seller and the maid to the hospital or somewhere else. Everyone knows that there is a morgue in Ayn Shaqq.

A Frenchman had the job of cracking the heads of the dead and cutting up their bodies. He always got drunk in the Capital Bar. He would get drunk alone, probably remembering all the skulls he cracked or the limbs he dismembered and played with. The flower seller was killed. The maid died and the deceased before them. He was well-dressed and polite and liked this and that. Of course, everyone likes this and that, then they get killed or they die, the way the black woman got killed and her maid died. There is definitely no difference between dying either way. One human life ends and another follows. For example, the flower seller's shop will be bought by someone else, the same goes for her house; no doubt another maid will come to clean the new house and the flower shop will be re-stocked with different kinds of flowers.

Some things go and some things stay. As flowers wilt so do souls inside their bodies. Souls may move from one body to another whether they are white, black or yellow. The black woman died, so did the maid, the deceased, and others. Their souls wilted exactly like flowers. They weaken and then they die. No one knew whether the black woman had any heirs. She lived with flowers, the dog, the abandoned church, the old women and the soul of the deceased. Did their two souls meet? No one knows. Everyone tries to stay around in this world. It is their right since they do not know what lies beyond. If they did they would all commit mass suicide to escape killings, starvation, sarcastic looks. Once the black flower seller told one of her friends: "Oh, if only we did not have eyes or ears!" The old Italian woman replied: "With our eyes we see and with our ears we hear." An old Moroccan woman married to an Austrian who had fought in the Second World War commented: "And we also have noses that smell the good and the rotten, and other things as well."

And in fact the flower seller did not try to hear or see or smell even the scent of her flowers. She was always quiet; she rarely spoke. If she heard anything, even if it concerned her, she would pretend otherwise and make no comment. Maybe the maid who killed her took her silence as a sign of stupidity. But she was not stupid, not in the way you imagine. The flowers beautifully arranged behind the shop window reflected her personality.

She did not talk a lot. When women talked about their husbands, she would only mention the well dressed and polite deceased, the dog and the flowers. She did not remember the names of her friends but she knew the names of the flowers she sold. She never named the deceased. Once one of her friends heard her mention the name Pedro. This friend told others that the flower seller was married to someone called Pedro.

One of them commented: "Her father must have been

black from one of the Spanish colonies."

"From Latin America," another said. "My late husband was born in Andalusia but he spent his childhood in Honduras. When his father died, he returned to Spain and joined the Reds, then deserted and married me. His name was Pedro, Pedro Gonzalez."

"Was he black?" a third asked.

"No, no, not at all! He was dark and beautiful and his one fault was that he loved women. Even so, I loved him. He was a real man who loved women. I believe that any real man has to love women."

Before her death the flower seller once said: "The deceased was a real man but did not love women much. He loved light drinks, boule and hunting wild boar. He stayed that way until he died."

"Was he your husband?"

She would remain silent or arrange some flowers and look through the window at the few passers-by or far away into an invisible world only she knew. Sometimes a tear would trickle down behind her thick glasses. At any rate, the deceased remained unknown to all those curious women who tried to know everything about the flower seller.

She died without anyone finding out about Pedro. No one ever saw Pedro even though they'd known her for a long time, and no man ever entered her home. She once said that he was good at cooking wild boar and how delicious the meat was and that Pedro found ways of preparing it. When the flower seller died no relative came to her house. No one was invited. Stranger still, no black man, child or woman came by her shop. Days later four people showed up. They opened the shop, its flowers had wilted; they pulled down the metal shutters, locked and sealed them with wax and documented something on some papers. They spoke among themselves and left.

Does a person's life begin and end in this way? This is what one of the teachers who lived in the same street thought.

Except that he did not have a relationship with flowers or animals. No one went to the funeral of the flower seller and no one knows how and where she was buried. They took her away in an ambulance and came back a few days later to seal up the shop. No one knows if she was buried in a Muslim, a Christian or a Jewish cemetery. The teacher thought: the main thing is that death is the same everywhere. There are those who are buried, those who are cremated, those who end up in the belly of the whale. Death is the same. Who will cry for whom? The one who grieves over the death of someone will in turn die tomorrow. He who leaves something behind will find someone else owning it without the least effort. Then he said: "I won't leave an inheritance for anyone." But then, what can a teacher who does not accept bribes leave behind?

Something has changed in the street since the death of the black flower seller. Her shop re-opened. Maybe another woman bought it. The one who spoke with a Fes accent and looked up at the sky as if the earth did not exist beneath her feet – the earth that she would be buried in some day. The shop would close again and get sealed with wax for a while. This is the end that meets you all.

*Translated by Mona Zaki*

# The Indian

## AHMAD BOUZFOUR

"Tell me a story."

He looked at me in surprise and said, smiling: "You are not a small boy."

"Tell me a story," I insisted.

He surveyed my face with a scrutinising look, measured my height and estimated my weight with his eyes, then looked at the cup of tea in my hand. He hesitated, then said: "A real or an imaginary story?"

"It doesn't matter."

"About grown-ups or little ones?"

"It doesn't matter."

"Well, then, I'll tell you a story, a real one about little ones since you are so old."

I believe I was not more than ten when I saw him for the first time. He was brown-skinned and his eyes were black, large, and calm. He himself was wholly calm: his eyes, his face, his slow movement when he walked, when he talked, when he laughed — no, I never saw him laugh — when he smiled, for he smiled often. Nothing could take him out of his peaceful calm, out of his confident composure — confident? I don't know. Sometimes I thought he was dull-witted or "cold-hearted", as my father once described him, so that if an earthquake happened, his seat would collapse under him and he would remain calm and peaceful as if he had ordered that. In the neighbourhood, they called him the Indian, I

191

don't know why. Because of his mulatto colour? Or because he worked with the Indians downtown? I believe he was originally from the south of the country, but his long, smooth, black hair and his large eyes and thick moustache that looked pitch-black next to his snow-white teeth gleaming between his thick, parted lips – all that, with his oil colour, suggested that one of his parents was a foreigner. But we knew nothing about him except that he had a room on the roof, that he worked with the Indians downtown, and that he liked children and told them stories.

To get rid of me one Sunday, my father ordered me to join the children in the company of the Indian and wait there for his return. In the afternoon, the Indian used to sit in the shade of the mosque wall with the children around him and he told them stories about Sindbad. That was the first time I sat before him and listened to him. I became fond of the Indian since that day and I hurried to him every Sunday afternoon, fascinated by his large, black eyes, his clean smile, his combed hair, his elegant attire, and his adventurous Sindbad.

There was no television in those days and even football did not attract us as passionately as it does children nowadays. I don't know, perhaps even stories would not have attracted us, had it not been for the Indian. We loved the sea, but the Indian rivalled it, and he wrenched his little audience from it with determination and persistence.

You know the stories of Sindbad, but he narrated them in a special way. No, it was not that theatrical way which acts out the tales and impersonates their heroes. He narrated the stories in a calm way that agreed with his calm temperament. The precise nature of his way was rather in its jumps. His narration was a succession of leaps, as if he were a small, timorous animal. He would stop for a moment, turn right and left, and then suddenly jump. He would pause again to justify and explain his jump, then he would fall silent, smiling and surveying us with his scrutinising look, and assessing the interest revealed in our eyes. And then he would suddenly jump again

. . . and so on and on.

For example, he would suddenly say without introduction: "And the djinn devoured Sindbad," and he would fall silent. How? Was that the end of the story? But he would continue, and he would explain that the djinn on the inside was as large as a city and that Sindbad, having been swallowed, roamed around like a tourist in the streets of the djinn's innards and discovered virgin lands full of fascinating, wonderful, strange things.

"And Sindbad ate the mountain," he would say and then fall silent. How? Had Sindbad become a djinn? But he would continue, and he would explain that the mountain was really made of candy, that its trees, birds, and animals were all sweetmeats and caramels, and that Sindbad spent seven years sucking the delicious mountain.

Oh, how delightful were the tales he told! However, I am not telling you now the story of Sindbad, but rather that of the Indian himself.

I was seventeen when I met him for the first time outside our neighbourhood. I saw him as I was wandering downtown. He was sitting at a café, his eyes following the passers-by with perspicacity and concentration as though he were voraciously eating the people's movements in the street. I looked at him for a long time from my position on the side. When he finally turned and saw me, he smiled and gestured to me with his hand. I sat next to him and he ordered coffee for me. When I asked him about his life, his smile widened and he calmly moved his large forefinger in front of my face and said: "Do you still like stories?"

I said I was asking him about his life.

He said: "What is the difference?"

He looked down at his shining shoes silently and then I heard him say: "It is related that there was a man in olden times who put a pebble in a glass for every good day that passed in his life. When he was asked how old he was, he emptied the glass and counted the pebbles. As for me, the first and last pebble I put in the glass was on the day I met Sindbad."

"You mean when you read the *Thousand and One Nights*?"

"No. I did actually meet Sindbad." He looked at me, smiling, and continued: "Sindbad does not die. He is like al-Khadir, the hidden Imam. He lives in all ages and with all generations: al-Khadir produces sciences and Sindbad produces stories."

"Well, how did you meet him?"

"I met him in a bar. In those days, I was addicted to drinking and we met over a glass as we sat at a table. My attention was drawn to the fact that, now and then, he wrote something on a Kleenex tissue. Whenever he took a sip, he wrote a line, then he folded the tissue and put it in his pocket. I asked him: 'What are you writing?' He said: 'One of my journeys.' I said: 'Take me with you.' He said: 'Come,' and he held my hand thus . . ."

(Suddenly, as the Indian stretched out his hand to hold mine, the cup of cold coffee spilled over the table and I found myself wrestling with a violent flow of turbulent, black waves as I tried to cling to consciousness. I screamed voicelessly, stretched out my hand, or tried to stretch it out, but it was as heavy as lead. Between my hand and the Indian's, which started to stretch out, then froze in that position of reaching out, there was a distance of thousands of kilometres of water, rising at times until the brown motionless large hand was covered. and subsiding at other times until the Indian's fingers emerged like stars . . . )

When I turned around, I found no one next to me.

The café was almost empty, the cup of tea on the table was almost empty, and my old friend telling me about Sindbad was no longer there. The sun turned yellow, the air began to cool down, and I felt the sweat on my forehead, cold and heavy like sea water. I took out the handkerchief from my pocket to wipe it off and a tissue fell out on the floor. I trembled in terror: A white Kleenex tissue . . . So, let it be . . . I opened the tissue on the table and began to read: "Jumm . . . and I jump, walkk . . . runnn . . . halala. . . balala, and be silent? How? And I write? And be quiet? How? And I solve? How? And they jummm. . . jummm . . . and I jump. Won't you jump? Look to the right . . . to the left . . . in front . . . behind . . . underneath . . . above . . . . Take care, jump, descend, turn around, look to the right, jump. It's an easy job, only observe them. Onlyly let them feel being observed, even if you've not observed them. Because I too feel I'm observed onlylyly. That's why I observe them, and I travel from here to there, from there to here, from here to here. And don't do anything: no report, no file, no pens, no notes, only from there to there, and observe them, . . . erve well otherwise . . .erve . . . erve. Jump, descend, turn around, obs . . . erve . . . erve also.

Finally, I was healed. To hell with them all: you, and they, and the others, you and they too, and I sat on the ground. Touch it with your sticky fingers. I touch it, feel it: pitch, the earth too is pitch. The earth said: "Pitttch, pitttch." I put my head between my hands, and I cried, pitch fell down from my eyes. A pool of pitch. Take off your clothes, piece by piece, the socks are a ship going out of Basra at dawn, get on board, the socks are a ship going out of Basra at dawn, get on board. India appears on the horizon, and he awaits you on the shore, so stretch out your hand. But he will erve-erve you, and will pounce on your dirty socks with why? how? where? when? whyyyy? . . . Aaaah . . . Your throat will split, let it split, and let it split split a thousand times plit. Who hears you in this halala balala . . . ?

The only solution is to drink, the only solution is to write, the only solution is to wake up, to erase consciousness, so that you may drink and write, so that you may express and bring ideas closer, so that you may fall into the sea and disappear, so write . . . ite."

And I stretched out my hand. . .

*Translated by Issa J Boullata*

195

# The Laws of Absence

## AHMED EL-MADINI

*This is what I'm looking for.*
*I have been looking for it,*
*yet running away from it.*

I do not know how a thing and its opposite can so coexist,
but such is my condition, forever unresolved, as we shall see.
Unresolved indeed, a state of being that is forever dependent
on its own becoming, an interim existence, a moment in
process that has yet to recognize its pastness or settle into its
futurity, a ceaseless whiling away of the interim trappings of
the now. Unrelenting, for ever and ever, until time itself
emerges, face on, rebellious and quizzical: What now? You
cannot escape what has come before me, nor can you evade
what is to come!

Such is my condition, facing it is like facing my own
impossibility, precisely as it becomes impossible for me to
interfere in the transpiring course of what has already happened, or what might happen, perhaps I could then rearrange
the events or redraw the faces or capture a passing thought,
no matter how impertinent.

To be able to tell of that which I've been at once looking
for and running away from, I must first get to know it, recognize it. I should at least somehow get nearer to it, near
enough to get a glimpse of it, a thread, a line, even a shadow.
Unable to do so, for it's hard to shorten distances where they

do not exist or discern dawning light when submerged in total darkness. Perhaps then I could just imagine it, in a sheer act of the imagination where what's real can expand itself. For the thing I'm looking for is there, an immanent in-between, wholly belonging to neither but partaking of both, not a mix but a piece of clay moulded as if of one and the same nature, out of which my flesh grew, covering my bones. The spirit?! Oh, how delicate is this spirit that I must at all times keep clinging to it, lest it slip away in between my lashes, myself out of myself lost forever!

I imagine I can retrieve the circumstances of my first birth by going through a second one, this time around a witness to the delivery both out of her womb and out of the womb of this world. There is of course a difference in these two instances, but I'm inclined to deny it, transcending this difference in the name of first presence, the first beginning of first forms, when I first screamed and never stopped screaming since then. Perhaps this will not obtain, neither physically possible nor immanently felt. But, just so you would know, I never once sought the understanding of others, as it's all but an illusion, nor have I ever sought favouring the indulgence of thousands. What there is to be gained from doing so is but soon spoilt, goes bad. Haa . . . yes, this is it, the word I'm looking for, and it's perhaps one of very few words left with which one can broach the subject.

Speech was beyond me before I could even begin to utter a word, it was beyond me to sail the high and dark seas of utterance, even when aided by metaphor . . . it has turned into a running river, then a raging ocean engulfing all, drowning even someone like me, who has known how to distil the nectar of speech, purify it, making it pristine again, primordial. But who can hold ground before the opened floodgates? Who can keep past promises? Promises long since made, to maintain forever the glory of speech, forever to let it spring forth from the heights, nonchalant, noble, witty, marching through the ages, luminous meanings lighting its skies, and in it a part of me is held, nay the whole of me, measured elegance, sweeping emotion, the spilling of words freshly conceived, rebelliousness the only language . . . and then gradually I begin to emerge, swerving into where I may rest into being, existing only where I can see but not be seen.

Now do you see how I burrowed my way closer, ever closer into a mode of discourse which I had not intended? Caught as if off guard. And so I'll speak for now about how I was so easily led in the direction of meanings, seething and seething and soon to cover me with their ashes, roaming about as if with no goal in sight, or delving deeper and deeper into myself, until words, braking out of age long self-reflection, begin to emerge as islets emerge from the ocean's depths, bellowing: What next? Here I am, I have come responding to a call you had promised to release, a cry, a dream, so long bent up and now is the time to unleash them, overpowering, war-like. But there is another dimension to this swerving mode of existence in which I find myself and which I seek to express through this need to delve deeper into something, let it be like the corn of a unicorn or the hole in the ground I suddenly see between my feet, swarming with ants, going in and out, completely oblivious of everything else, eternally so.

I tell him "Free me, Have mercy and relax your reigns". I am tired of ever crouching, ever so lying down and stretching into dimension after dimension before I can get to rest in the essence. How long has it been, how many lines, how many ages, have I been plagued with constantly oscillating in the nearness of your proximities? I have taken you by force only that once, when I released you at the entrance to my labyrinth. But you have overtaken me a thousand times over as you carved your words in the mirrors of burning amazement stretched on before you and as I kept asking and asking, propelled with the questioning into this labyrinth. Shsh . . . I can actually hear the sound of my footsteps, pressing like hooves and etching over my body the messages of generations destined to forgetfulness. He persists in his exaggerated callousness, his penchant for haughtiness, even his garbled banalities. But I insist on not forgetting, I shall pursue remembrance until I have exorcised him, until I have become one other than him: Speech.

*This isn't what I have been looking for.*
*But it is what I do not know how to escape from.*

The book has many chapters, and I have but times and locales that have pierced me after etching with sharp needles their painful signs and raising their edifices, standing edifices or crumbling ones . . . and then these times and places began to recede, returning to where they came from, leaving me neither inside them nor outside. Let us then bid for what to name this pristine, original spot. Let us give it skies, a moon and eternally shining stars, and populate it with creatures made of clay that's a mix of all other creatures. Let us up the anti and say these creatures will speak in hitherto unspoken tongues, and their utterance shall have no sound nor accent but that kind of sign which permeates all of nature. And every once in a while I shall be able to exchange a few signs in an attempt to impart to them the sensation that it's foolish to try and leave this pristine spot and that what lies outside is but absolute exile.

But I find myself wavering in my desire to search for a name. Were I to go any further I should have to find myself the prisoner of the magical lamp of perishing names. I must first brace myself before facing the barrage of jeering calls and shouted insults, before I find myself standing at the gates of history, in its beginnings, trying to stare afresh into faces that have gone before me and determined my humanity in the name of history, spotting none that looked like mine, none that betrayed the features of a whole genealogy fashioned by me out of dreaming breath. Tragically I must leave them behind to face extinction, all alone, as I take the irretrievable step. And when my name confronts me in full view I shall declare in its presence my desire for hastening it into oblivion, that we may journey together and be ushered into another memory, as vast as the expanse of absence that engulfs me and extends beyond the bounds of earth. Ah, me . . . how will I gather together my limbs and concentrate my body, that with open breast I can house your absence?

My hearing impaired, a veil drawn over my vision, words perching as if in thick clouds over my lips, here lying, neither soaring nor withdrawing, neither boldly venturing nor retreating, never sought by me nor do I know how to run to it seeking refuge from it. What unspeakable state do I find myself in? No one will come to my rescue, for no one is capable of overtaking this vast absence while standing on two feet watching countries and peoples as they crumble down and collapse into each other. There is no escape for me from this horror, my hearing impaired, a veil drawn over my vision. I draw back my stretched arms and posture as if a latter-day Sphinx, but I shall forthwith begin to learn the alphabet of silence, for then perhaps I can find the path that leads to you.

One long stretch, lonely, wild, and no road signs nor guides. No moonshine casting its silver on the way, no pigeon cooing nor the sound of pond frogs. The path is where we tread from point to point, and without this treading it turns into a straight line or a line meandering in the distance, or the absolute. I know my starting point, or at least I presume the knowledge given the sensation I have of this overwhelming, voluminous absence. But I do not know my destination, not at all, as if a traveller had just booked a one-way ticket to an unknown destination. I have travelled a great deal in my life and arrived at many remote destinations, not out of curiosity, for a single city suffices as the beloved city; no, it was not so much that as the constant fleeing from one place to the next as if chased, and in an interminable search for what I knew not.

No one around, almost no one – only faces that began to lose their features after so many encounters, not suspecting that the intensity of seeing erases what is seen, retaining only the peculiarity of its own act. The path is long, endlessly stretching before you, and into the horizon stretches yet another path, and your problem becomes your dilemma over the confidence in the immediate step and the longing to arrive there and, in between, your frustration over walking over a path you have not chosen. A pre-determined path on which you find yourself even though you're still outside those who shake their heads as they pass you by under the pretext of companionship. Suddenly they disappear, their statures and their shadows, swept over, and in the air around what do you see but scattered bits or raised dust, the possible remains of a possible existence that has just passed.

You decide to come to a halt, you pound the ground firmly with your feet, making sure it is still holding under you, each hand takes hold of the other, measuring its beat, preparing for a journey that will begin on a path that has come to view and not come to view. You say you are on it and yet you retreat. Those holding the fort up the path think you are fleeing from them, they think they scare you; what, can a swarming murkiness of vermin be so feared? You begin to feel the earth losing its patience, even feel disgusted by such as those who hopelessly walk its face. You see its face contorting into a frown as sudden wrinkles begin to invade it. Only a moment ago did you see its face cheerful, blooming as in spring the fields stretching between Rabat and Mèknes. Beneath me the earth began to speak, through the pores of my skin, to the intoxication of the soil and I could sense all birds near and far holding their breath so that only its singing could be heard . . . but soon you shall listen and you shall see what language it speaks, you shall . . .

I rushed toward her, having attached myself firmly to its many ancient trunks. I need warmth and sustenance, said I, before I embark on a path I haven't chosen. I have consecrated myself to her, not out of need. I said this to her among the many other things I said as the warm current of magnetism resulting from our intimate proximity began to increase in intensity. As I began to move even closer to her sweet slumber, all my senses honed in, a greeting had already paved the way for me, perhaps more the sign of maddening love than a greeting. Perhaps she had then cleared the space next to her, motioning me into her nearness . . . her shadow my bedding and the exuding warmth of her cheek my pillow. I rested my head next to her, pulling over us an ancient winter's rain cloud which brought back the memory of sweet longing.

I rushed toward her burning with love, holding dearly to my sorrows and her slumber, as she gathered to herself sparse flesh and bone and as one gathers dry twigs for fire she began to gather the remains of a seeing that has tarried for long around corners and pulled down drapes of time over walls, time that is hers, time that has known both the inside and the outside. Over the drapes were dancing shadows. Spectres? Ghosts? Shadows of a lived life? How can memory possibly contain all of it? These are my own shadows, I almost screamed, and I am that spectre, all of it, or part of it, that trembling reflection in a mirror that's running away from the rustiness of life? That's me, one with her, part for whole, as I stretch out my arm reaching with a measuring hand, and her hand as out of me reaching out. She ruffles my hair as I begin to feel an electric current of tickles all over. Oh, how sweet my life becomes then! Who is left for me after she's gone? Oh, how far away she feels now . . .

But we shall surely remain connected. I shall bring you closer to me, make you closeness itself. I have spread all over, long and thin, and now is the time to call back to me my own separations, asking forgiveness for all my whims, my lifetime follies no longer wearing me straight as a sword, as you have always known me. You have always wished me to remain close, I who have been at one with the stretching of distances. And when I had resigned myself to renouncing my exilic state, what we had covered or were about to cover of the way together began to seem even more remote. Yet have I sought you out as far as your own extreme, and plunged as deep as your roots, hoping as if from a rose to absorb all your nectar, not giving thought to how mother earth feeds on nostalgia, once eyes wide open, awake, and once . . .

*No. This is not what I have been looking for.*
*It is as though I were giving in to it just when my desire is to run away from it.*

My desire seems to have its own private plans. Yes, this is more like it. My desire too seeks to become independent of me, just as those words which I think are issued by me, strung by my own will and design to fit into patterns and forms which I or someone else calls my style. The fact of the matter is that each word has its own history and genealogy, and it has its place even before it reaches me, and after. No one can afford to reign in language, any language, no one can any longer control that which has no beginning or end.

I shall pretend that I possess language, while of course I do not know how to do it. Nay, I can feel it coursing through my body as if in blood streams whose circulation is but forgotten, the way I have forgotten a name that's forever attached to me, until someone calls me by it. And why not. When someone mentions it to me I realize all of a sudden that we make such a strange couple, and yet a serious decoupling: over there myself and over there language, each claiming to master the other as each declares total independence. And yet we remain the one tied to both, and to the one that it is. Exactly the way I am not my own name. Someone wants to fix me in it, to imprison me in the shaping of its letters, each letter a wall, utterance the ceiling, calling the gate. I am an Other, and whoever wishes to call this a splitting of personality, a revelling in schizophrenia, let them do so, I do not mind, not for as long as I have shaken off their pious drive for oneness.

I pondered long over the difference and over this exegetical feat, hoping thus to climb slowly and peacefully toward her station, seeking her the way a Sufi seeks his goal, the folds of my speech covering tattoos carefully etched out of some of that with which she has named me, perhaps more perhaps less. We may at times hit the thought that perhaps we could dispel some of the loneliness by addressing each other in hith-erto unknown words, in a language whose alphabet will have just been invented and with every sound uttered, one moves closer to existing. When I rushed to her my arms were strain-ing before me in her direction, my hands were all ears for the fresh language you're teaching and I began to stretch between us as fresh land, struck by an intuition for things that will transpire only with that intuition, for as long as it lasts. I real-ized then that the journey is a long one and the road to her is that which goes through her. What do I do then if this is the only road and she flees from it? With her and through her I try to raise her name once more over the ruins of my for-getfulness, and for the sake of this raging fire . . . raging for memory.

She withdraws into her absence even when fully present before my eyes, the distance between us as long as the next step. Or so I estimated. Have I not been firm with other steps made in the past? Once more, my opinion will contradict my feelings, but I shall persist in my contradictions until all meaning is exhausted. We shall remain thus in this eternal recurrence, surrendering to similitude as it recreates our faces and speech and buries them in concave mirrors that are but mere words. But the letters shall grow small crowns, I say, and the next scene wherein we embrace, I will transfix with my inner sight, and none of those utterly empty words will be able to steal it away. She made a motion which I interpreted to be the signal for quickening stagnant waters, but then it was her silence, in which she dwells, that reigned as I stood uncomprehending, and unable to reach out my hands and with my moving fingers shatter it.

Silence has many forms, shades, many titles, many names. Rich in meaning and advantageous all around, towering high and yet lying stiff as a corpse, a sturdy body and a vanishing ghost. It is what descends to the bottomless pit of planets and what parts the young lips of girls as they eye the first sign of swelling bosom, the first letter in the alphabet of crystallizing dew and the last sigh of the last crimson of sunset, dawn as it breaks on you and evening repose as it collapses exhausted on the bench. Silence speaks in many tongues and is redolent with metaphor, the last of which a posted letter that never reaches you for the brevity of speech has reached the point of extinction. I begin to rub the whiteness of the blank sheet, hoping to elicit speech, but to no avail. It has the shaky diffidence of first love and stubbornly slipped into the dark recesses of its silence. I heard myself listening in on my uttered words as they loosened from my tongue only to be delivered to my own hearing. For this earth my mother has turned in, measuring what is left of her beats with inward-turning eyelids, as if to bid me farewell, while I fancied my eyes wide open receiving daylight.

Silence offers the name which she will choose for her journey, and for this image in which she appears shrouded with the murky silver of transparent mist, her body stretched out, the mistress of none. Life and death equally recoiled before her repose. I am certain she will rise despite her burning lungs and despite the fatal arrows which seek their defining destiny in her. Silence too offered the air of bewilderment that surrounded her as we stood there staring in bewilderment, awaiting the moment when she retrieves her inward hiddenness and on the surface lets open a portal for us through which we can glimpse a hint of her majesty. She, in the end, has the unnamable silence defying all attribution, beyond naming, defiant in the face of all, and in whose ingratiating inimitability her story has unravelled: through her I shall come, she who is the one to come before me.

And then I was made nearer by a call, calling on me to return in haste to where I know not where I was before. She wants you and you alone, the voice commanded, She has covenants and you are the entrusted one. Who is she? I asked. Our mother earth, Your mother, the voice answered impatiently, How could it be, have you forgotten? I knew not what to answer and swallowed up my silence. I have one of two choices and no possibility of choosing: either I burst out wailing and the universe trembles in echo, or the letters relent and give way out of awe for what they harkened unto, since no one had forewarned me before the calling and so I was distracted away from them. Up until then I had taken up residence in the city of heedlessness, moving quarters many a time, until springs of forgetfulness began to gush out of me, or nearly so. I never heeded the possibility of extinction, ceasing to exist never frightened me, but to survive in this abyss, among these scowling faces that have discoloured the face of day, young leaves withering and falling under their gaze . . . But the calling has finally arrived.

I found people of mixed origins standing before her gates, I did not know who they were, nor was there rejoicing in their faces, I took it as a bad omen. Traditionally the roads are made accessible and thresholds are laid open as I approach, what then with this gloominess that almost it has itself almost become a sure sign of the times? I overheard someone addressing or referring to a person who has had gone too deep into absence, what am I to do with him? She had waited far too long for him but he never showed up, and so she held his face tightly with the palms of her hands, and as someone seeking blessings she rubbed her chest with his image as she intoned the verse "Have we not gladdened your heart?" Indeed. It was as though she had reached out for me with open arms, but it was an illusion to imagine her thus or to imagine her lying by my side. Another retorted, how could he be in love with her and yet spurn her thus, and then she would decide to become forever absent, that the fire of love raging within her would never go out? We hear not the sounds from her inner dwelling, he then added, and we have heard that once she had so betaken herself she turned into an ascetic; and no one but him can lure her out of her asceticism. Now that she is gone, who will relieve us of our burden, where shall we find a countenance like hers that will show us the way?

Another and yet another arrived. Those who came were many. Silence all around began to intensify and coalesce into a dark cloud, and in every throat a choking question. People hailed from far away places, and now they have arrived, only to find no one waiting for them and no one among them had the answer to the question "Who summoned us hither?". Who tore us away from our familiar abode of forgetfulness?

A venerable old sheikh roamed the place swinging an incense burner, softening the air with sweet incense, as the sound of Qur'anic recitation filling the air issued from the depth of a back room. Down a long corridor, which led to an invisible interior, a man passed balancing on his head a long wooden board such as the one used for delivering kneaded bread dough to the baker's, followed by a coterie of women carrying pots and saucepans amongst which were two filled with honey and oil. The growing tree of questioning also produced fruit: What is the meaning of all these goings and comings, all this incense and recitation, the overriding gloominess, and this anguished suspense hanging in the air like unrelieved clouds? What does it mean for me thus to stand before all these people, speechless, neither crying nor mourning nor . . .

How could he have so forgotten about me, she wondered, or is it that time just slipped through his fingers coursing in veins of shyness or forgetfulness? I said to him, Come to me, Come in my dreams; longing for him by day is hurting enough, surely there's hope in my long, sleepless nights. Perhaps I spread too high and far into the horizon, when I sent the outer limits of my dreams in chase after the sweet aroma of his advent, so near to me, Come, to me, the high and luminous bearing of light displaying all shades and intensities, Come, to me . . . you, Oh, son of tempestuousness and passion, how could you endure my absence? Man or woman, who could provide the like of my kiss on your cheek, who pulls you to the like of my embrace, who overtakes you thus? Who has the promise of many more such embraces, saved for you after your life long exile? You shall bear your love on you, and as I know you, you shall ride it like a tempestuous, raging wind. One fleeting glimpse, and my long departure shall pour down torrential from my night skies.

The dark portals of night opened out one after the other, as did the galleries of day, and all meaning roamed about stranded, without shelter. I had resigned myself to bearing about my loss as a badge, and I donned the costume of such as this country, proudly swaddled in the garbs of futility. Previously I had been split in half, torn between the echoes of memory and the whirlpool of ardent wish, Where are you to be found, oh unspoken secret of my life and womanly sign of my end? Where might you be found? Is it my vertigo that sends me into vertiginous questioning and leaves me only its winged thoughts fluttering whilst you stand before me, your face veil upon veil as if other to itself, as if I could no longer comprehend its many multiplying features? But out of these eyes, perpetually receding from me, today flash the springs of signs, and each sign leads me to anywhere but away from you, all whilst you stand right here, stretching as far as the earth and as wide as the skies, whilst you remain here.

I have come but to a late arrival after my longing journeying after you, and at the gates of longing for you I found many waiting there, all volunteers to carry the emblems of waiting and the signs of your reproval. No matter what they believed, none of them matched me, none had my ancient standing outside your door, nor my ability to detect the scent of your early departure, despite your ever remaining here, sitting, standing, by me, to my side, before me, around me, all around, and silence reigning in our diffident, awed expressions, ever outspoken, betraying our passion, the one for the other, and that other yet for another, for whom it reaches out and by whom it returns. That's why no matter what they thought none of them matched me, for when I departed I departed not to any place but to where you are, remaining in you, seeing and not believing that you were departing.

Toward the end, four men were hailed to go in, then two were gone and the other two remained. I had never seen the like of these two men before. They are no doubt human, but the way they cast their looks and the manner of their dress betray them for who they are, strangers. They neither affirmed nor denied, not saying Yes or No, never extended a greeting, never spoke in words, they only hinted that they were in haste for the matter to be decided and done with, the die to be cast. Suddenly they sprang wings and began to hover directly above us, and it became clear to me how adept they were. Some time passed as we watched baffled, awestruck, as they hovered performing what looked like a dance or twisting and turning in the space above us, which began to expand as they circulated above where she lay on the floor. We were even more amazed as stars began to shine and as we listened to what seemed to be a trail of divine praise descending upon them, as had never been reported before, and then, God as my witness, I saw a procession passing through as a meteor in the sky.

It came to pass then that these two were gone and the two departed were back. This time we could see them. They had appeared while we were under the spell of the flying scene, and so entered unnoticed by us, emerging from the inside of the spiral, one taking the lead as the other followed, and stretched between the two there appeared a bed of green. We could not tell who lay on it, but we lowered our eyes humbly and piously as he passed. We could only discern the greenness all around, so lush and deep it had grown all around us taking every form and shape of tree leaves, green leaves. I was all in perplexity then. Do I proceed to join the departing procession? Or should I move inward where I must enter the deep room and bow down before the laid out body?

*Translated by Ayman El-Desouky*

# THE AUTHORS

LATIFA BAQA was born in Sale, Morocco. She has a BA in Sociology from the Mohammed V University, Rabat. In 1992, she was awarded the Prize of the Union of the Writers of Morocco for young short story writers for her first collection *Ma allathi Naf'alu? [What is it that We Do?]*. She has two collections of short stories, published by Anwal and the Union of the Writers of Morocco.

AHMED BOUZFOUR was born in 1945 in Taza, Morocco. He studied Arabic Literature, and lectures at the College of Literature and Humanities in Casablanca. Starting publishing in the 1970s, he has published seven collections of short stories and a book of essays on pre-Islamic poetry. He is a leading short story writer in the Arab world. In 2004 he refused the award of a prize by the Ministry of Culture in protest at the lack of government policies to tackle the problems facing young Moroccans.

RACHIDA EL-CHARNI was born in Tunis. She started publishing her short stories in Arab magazines and newspapers in 1990. She published her first collection in 1997. Her second collection, in 2000, was awarded First Prize for the Arab Women's Creative Writing Prize in Abu Dhabi, but only after the ruling by censors that she change the title *God Loves Me, Credo* (one of the stories). In 2002, a new complete edition was published in Beirut, with a new title *Saheel al-As'ila [The Neighing of Questions]* and the inclusion of the censored story.

MOHAMED CHOUKRI (15 July 1935 – 15 November 2003) is one of Morocco's great contemporary writers, known mainly for his debut novel *For Bread Alone* that was published first in

211

English, translated by Paul Bowles, in 1973 after being banned by the Moroccan government. It was eventually published in Arabic in 1982. The book broke taboos in the Arab world, being a stark autobiographical novel of a young street kid's struggle to survive and get an education.

MOHAMMED DIB (1920-2003) was born in Tlemcen, Algeria. He was educated in Oudja, just across the border in Morocco. He wrote poems and painted from an early age. During the 1940s he worked as teacher, accountant, interpreter (English and French), and designer. Active as a militant and a journalist in the war for independence, he was forced into exile, and settled permanently in France in 1964. His powerful epic trilogy *Algerie*, was published in France between 1952 and 1957, followed by many other novels, collections of short stories and poems, plays, essays and children's stories. He remains one of the best known of Algerian francophone writers.

TAREK ELTAYEB was born in Cairo of Sudanese parents. He studied at Ain Shams University, Cairo, and has been living in Vienna since 1984. He has a PhD from the University of Vienna on the transfer of ethics through technology. He has published three volumes of short stories and a novel, *Towns without Palm Trees*, which has been published in French and German.

MANSOURA EZELDIN was born in 1976 in a small village in Delta Egypt. She graduated in Journalism from the University of Cairo in 1998, later working in Egyptian television. She is currently a journalist on the literary magazine *Akhbar al-Adab*. She started publishing her short stories in the Arab press in 1997. In 2001 her first collection *Dhaw'a Muhtaz [Shaken Light]* came out, and in 2004 her first novel *Matahat Meryam [Meryam's Labyrinth]*. Some of her work has been translated to French and German.

GAMAL EL-GHITANI was born at Sohag, upper Egypt, in 1945, and grew up in Cairo. A novelist, short story writer and journalist, he is currently editor of the influential Cairo weekly, *Akhbar al-Adab*. His first book of short stories, *The Papers of a Young Man who has lived for a Thousand Years*, established his literary talent. He has written nine novels, including the landmark of modern Arabic fiction, the post-modern and allegorical *Al-Zayni Barakat* (1974), which has been translated into ten languages. It was the first modern Arabic novel to be published by Penguin Books; it was republished by AUC Press in 2004. He has also published a major three-volume novel *Al-Tajaliyyat* (published in 2005 in French translation), and many collections of short stories, several now in their second and third editions, with a number translated into English, French, German, Spanish, Italian and Hebrew.

SAID AL-KAFRAWI was born and brought up in a village in Delta Egypt. He has published eight collections of short stories, and one selection published in English, *The Hill of Gypsies and Other Stories,* translated by Denys Johnson-Davies. Some of his works have been translated into several other languages.

IDRISS EL-KHOURI was born in Casablanca, Morocco, in 1939. Since the early 1960s he has published eight collections of short stories and two volumes of essays. He worked as a journalist until his retirement, and is a major figure in modern Moroccan literature.

AHMED EL-MADINI was born in Casablanca, Morocco, in 1948. He is a graduate of the University of Fes, and worked first as a teacher in his home town. He has published eight collections of short stories, eight novels and two volumes of poetry and five columes of cultural essays, one in French (Hachette, 1994). In 2002, he broke away from the Moroccan Union of Writers, and founded the League of Moroccan Writers, of which he is Secretary-General.

ALI MOSBAH was born in 1953 in Zaghwan, Tunisia. He studied social sciences at the Sorbonne, Paris, and Philosophy and Social Sciences in Berlin. He taught in Tunis secondary schools from 1980 to 1989, and then settled in Berlin, Germany, where he still lives. He has published short stories and essays in many Arab quarterlies, and has one travel book, *Cities and Faces,* which won the Ibn Battuta Prize in Abu Dhabi in 2004. Some of his short stories have been translated to French and German. He has translated works of Nietsche to Arabic.

HASSOUNA MOSBAHI was born in Kairouan, Tunisia, in 1950, and is a novelist, critic and freelance journalist in the German press, having lived in Munich from 1985 to 2004 when he returned to Tunisia. In 2000 he won the Munich Fiction Prize for the German translation of his novel, *Tarshish Hallucination*. He has published, in Arabic and German, four volumes of short stories, two novels, a travel book and some non-fiction.

SABRI MOUSSA was born in Dumyat, Egypt, in 1932, and now lives in Cairo. He has published four collections of short stories, three novels, three travel books and scripts for ten major Egyptian films, including the classic film *al-Bustagi [The Postman]*.

MUHAMMAD MUSTAGAB comes from Daryut, a village in Upper Egypt. He was involved with the construction of the High Dam before turning to journalism. He has published three collections of short stories and two novels. He has won several Egyptian literary prizes.

HASSAN NASR was born in Tunis in 1947, and has been publishing his works since 1969. He studied Arabic Literature and Language in Tunis and Baghdad and lived for many years in Mauritania. He was a high school teacher, and has published novels and collections of short stories, all dealing powerfully with daily life. He won particular acclaim for his semi-autobiographical novel *Dar al-Basha*. He lives in Tunis, and is a leading figure in contemporary Tunisian literature.

RABIA RAIHANE is from Morocco. She was a teacher of Arabic language and literature, and now works for the Ministry of National Education. She was awarded First Prize for Arab Women's Creative Writing in Abu Dhabi, and has three collections of short stories. Some of her stories have been translated into French, German and Spanish.

TAYEB SALIH was born in Northern Sudan in 1929 and educated at the University of Khartoum. He was briefly a teacher and then worked in the Arabic Service of the BBC in London. He has been Director General of Information Services in Qatar, worked with UNESCO in Paris and as UNESCO's Representative in the Arab Gulf States. He is recognised as one of the most important contemporary Arab writers and his *Season of Migration to the North* was selected by a panel of Arab writers and critics as the most important Arab novel of the twentieth century.

HABIB SELMI was born in al-'Ala, Tunisia, in 1951. He has published five novels and two collections of short stories. Many of his short stories have been translated into English and other languages. His first novel, *Jabal al-'Anz [Goat Mountain],* was published in French in 1999, and his second *Ushaq Bayya [Bayya's Lovers]* in 2003. He has lived in Paris since 1983.

IZZ AL-DIN AL-TAZI was born in Fes, Morocco, in 1948. He teaches in Tatwan. He started publishing his work in 1966 in Arabic quarterlies and newspapers. In 1975 he published his first short story collection, and in 1978 his first novel was published in Baghdad. He has published to date thirteen novels and collections of short stories.

MOHAMMED ZEFZAF (1945-2001) was born in Souq Arbiya' al-Gharb, Morocco. In his youth he wrote poetry, but soon turned to narrative. In the first years of Independence he moved to Rabat and then Casablanca, writing modern works of daily life that were to become well known throughout the Arab literary world, among them his novel *Al-Mara'a wal-Wardah [The Lady and the Rose].* A journalist and critic since the 1960s, Zefzaf published eighteen novels and collections of short stories. He was considered one of the masters of short story writing in contemporary Arabic literature.

# THE TRANSLATORS

ALI AZERIAH was born in Morocco and holds a degree in Translation and Linguistics from the University of Bath, UK, and a PhD in Comparative Literature and Translation Studies fromSUNY-Binghamton, NewYork. He teaches translation and translation theory at King Fahd School of Translation, Tangiers, Morocco.

AIDA A BAMIA is Professor in the Department of African and Asian Languages and Literatures at the University of Florida, USA. She is a regular contributor to *Banipal*.

ISSA J BOULLATA is a Palestinian writer, literary critic and translator. He is Professor of Arabic Literature at McGill University, Montreal, Canada. He is the author of *Trends and Issues in Contemporary Arab Thought* (1990), *Modern Arab Poets 1950-1975*, many other works; also several short stories and a novel in Arabic *Homecoming to Jerusalem* (1998). He has translated books by Jabra Ibrahim Jabra, Mohamed Berrada, Emily Nasrallah and Ghada Samman. He is a Contributing Editor of *Banipal*.

PETER CLARK worked for the British Council in the Arab world from the 1960s to the 1990s. He is the author of *Marmaduke Pickthall British Muslim* (1986) and his eighth translation from Arabic, *The Woman of the Flask* by Salim Matar is being published in 2005 by the American University in Cairo Press. He is a Contributing Editor of *Banipal*.

AYMAN EL-DESOUKY is a Lecturer in Arabic at the School for Oriental and African Studies, London. He has taught at Harvard and at Johns Hopkins Universities in the USA. His field is nineteenth and twentieth century Arabic and contemporary literature and literary theory.

NADA ELZEER was born in Lebanon. She holds an MPhil in European Literature from the University of Cambridge, UK, and is pursuing a PhD in Arabic Terminology at the University of Durham, UK. She has taught Arabic at the University of Durham and currently teaches Islamic studies at the University of Sunderland.

JAMES KIRKUP is a poet, novelist, dramatist and translator. He has written travel books about Asia and the United States and has published numerous volumes of poetry, including *No More Hiroshimas, A Correct Compassion, The Descent into the Cave, The Prodigal Sons, Refusal to Conform* and *The Body Servant*. His *A Book of Tanka* was awarded the Japanese Festival Foundation Prize in 1996, and he won the Scott Moncrieff Prize for literary translation in 1995. He has translated several African authors and Japanese poets. He is a regular contributor to *Banipal*.

SHAKIR MUSTAFA is assistant professor in the Department of Modern Foreign Languages and Literatures at Boston University, USA. He grew up in Iraq and received his BA and MA from Baghdad University in the early 1970s, teaching at Mosul University 1979-1990. He has a PhD from Indiana University (1999) teaching there 1991–2000 and co-editing of *A Century of Irish Drama* (Indiana University Press, 2000). He is a regular contributor to *Banipal*.

WEN-CHIN OUYANG was born in Taiwan, brought up in Libya and studied in the United States, gaining a PhD in Arabic Literature from Columbia University. She currently lectures in classical Arabic at the School of African and Asian Studies, London. She is the author of *Literary Criticism in Medieval Islamic Culture: The Making of a Tradition* (1997).

REBECCA PORTEOUS has translated work by Emily Nasrallah and has worked in publishing, and as a journalist in Cairo.

MOHAMMED SHAHEEN is Jordanian, the Vice-President of Mut‘ah University, Jordan. He has a PhD from the University of

Cambridge, and teaches literary criticism, twentieth century English and Comparative Literature. Among his many publications in English are a study of the impact of T S Eliot on modern Arabic poetry, *The Modern Arabic Short Story* (2003) and *E.M. Forster and The Politics of Imperialism* (2004).

PAUL STARKEY read Arabic and Persian Language and literature at Oxford University, and now heads the Department of Arabic at Durham University. He has written a critical study on Tawfiq Hakim, co-edited the *Encyclopaedia of Arabic Literature* and among others, has translated Rashid al-Daif's *Dear Mr Kawabata* and Edwar al-Kharrat's *The Stones of Bobello* (2005). He is working on a study of the Egyptian 'generation of the sixties'. He is a regular contributor to *Banipal*.

MONA ZAKI is Egyptian and was born in Belgrade, Yugoslavia. She has a BA from the American University in Cairo in Middle East history. She is completing a PhD on the medieval Muslim depiction of Hell at Princeton University. She is a Contributing Editor of *Banipal*.

# ACKNOWLEDGEMENTS & SOURCES

The publisher thanks Steve Porter of Westwords and the London Borough of Hammersmith and Fulham for the support which has made the publication of this volume of North African stories possible. Thanks also to Sarah Macalaster for all her help in its production.

The publisher thanks all the authors, the thirteen translators and all the original publishers who have given their permission to republish stories translated and published in issues of *Banipal*, as noted below, from the following original works:

LATIFA BAQA: "BAD SOUP!" was first published in *Banipal* No 19 from her collection of short stories *Ma Allathi Naf 'aluh? [What Is It We Do?]*, Moroccan Union of Writers, Rabat, 1992

AHMAD BOUZFOUR: "The Indian" was first published in *Banipal* No 5 and is from his short story collection *Diwan al-Sindbad*, published in 1995.

RACHIDA AL-CHARNI: "The Furnace" [Al-Furn] and "Life on the Edge" were first published in *Banipal* No 10/11 and are from the same collection of short stories, the latter being the title story of the collection *al-Hayat ala Haffat al-Dunya*, Dar al-Maaref, Sousse, Tunisia, 1997.

MOHAMED CHOUKRI: "Men Have All the Luck" [Al-Rijal Mahadhoudhoun], written in March 1967, is translated from his collection *Al-Kayma*, published by Al-Kamel Verlag, Köln, Germany, 2000. It is published in *Banipal* No 22 and in this selection by kind permission of the late author's agent Roberto de Hollanda and estate.

MOHAMMED DIB: "The Companion" was first published in *Banipal* No 7 with the author's permission, and is from his short story collection *Au Café*, published by Babel, Actes Sud, Paris,1996. It is published in this selection by kind permission of the estate of Mohammed Dib and Actes Sud.

TAREK ELTAYEB: "The Sweetest Tea with the most Beautiful Woman" was first published in *Banipal* No 21, Autumn 2004 and is from the author's short story collection, *Al-Gamal La Yaqif Khalfa Ishara Hamra*, Al-Hadara Publishing House, Cairo, 1993.

MANSOURA EZELDIN: "Butrus: A Distant Hazy Face" was first published in *Banipal* No 22 and is from the author's short story collection *Dhaw'a Muhtaz [Shaken Light]*, Cairo, 2001.

GAMAL EL-GHITANI: "Al-Mahsool"["The Crop"] was first published in *Banipal* No 21 and was translated from a special short stories edition of *Kitaab al-'Arabi*, No 24, Kuwait, 1989.

SAIDAL-KAFRAWI: These two short stories were first published in *Banipal* No 9. "Provisions of Sand" [Zad min rimal] is from the author's collection *Sidrat al-Muntaha*, Dar al-Ghad, Cairo, 1990, and "A Plait for Maryam" [Jadilat li-Maryam] from his short story collection *Dawa'ir min Hanin*, Dar Toubqal, Casablanca, 1997.

IDRISS EL-KHOURI: "Black and White" was first published in *Banipal* No 5 and is from the author's short story collection *Dhilal [Shadows]*, Casablanca.

AHMED EL-MADINI: "The Laws of Absence" was first published in *Banipal* No 20 and is from his latest short story collection *Huruf al-Zain*, Rabat, 2002.

ALI MOSBAH: "Wind" was first published in *Banipal* No 22, Spring 2005, translated from its online publication in www.kikah.com.

HASSOUNA MOSBAHI: "The Tortoise" was first published in *Banipal* No 6, and is the title story from the collection of short stories *Al-Sulhufa*, Dar Gilgamesh, Paris 1996. In 2001 it was shortlisted for the Caine Prize for African Writing .

SABRI MOUSSA: "Sa'diya Fell from the Balcony" and "Rasmiya! Your Turn is Next" were first published in *Banipal* No 8.

MUHAMMAD MUSTAGAB: "Hulagu" was first published in *Banipal* No 12, and is from the author's collection of short stories, *Dayrut al-Sharif,* Maktabat Madbuli, Cairo, 1986. The title "Hulagu" refers to the Mongol leader Hulagu (c 1217-65), Genghis Khan's grandson and founder of the Il-Khan empire in the Middle East.

HASSAN NASR: "Thawr Khallafahu Abi" [My Father's Ox] was first published in *Banipal* No 19, Spring 2004 and is from the author's short story collection *Layali al-Matar [Nights of Rain]*, first published in 1968. This translation is from the new edition published by Dar al-Yamama, Tunis.

RABIA RAIHANE: "A Red Spot" was first published in *Banipal* No 22, and published in Arabic in *Al-Quds* newspaper.

TAYEB SALIH: "If She Comes" is from the short story collection *Doumat wid Hamid* in the author's collected works, published by Dar al-Awda, Beirut, 1996. This translation published in *Banipal* No 22 and in this selection with kind permission of the author and his agent.

HABIB SELMI: "The Visit" was first published in *Banipal* No 4 and translated from its publication in *Al-Karmel* magazine, Cyprus, 1990.

IZZ AL-DIN AL-TAZI: "The Myth of the North" was first published in *Banipal* No 5 and is from the author's collection of short stories *al-Shababik [The Windows]*, Al-Boukili Publishing, Kunaitra, Morocco 1996.

MOHAMMED ZEFZAF: These two stories were first published in *Banipal* No 9. "Sardeen wa burtuqal" is from the author's collection of short stories *Al-'Araba*, Dar 'Ukadh, Rabat 1993. "The Flower Seller" is the title story of Zefzaf's collection of short stories *Bai'at al-Ward*, Dar 'Ukadh, Rabat, 1996.